CW01402125

TWELVE TALES
of
GOOD WOMEN
and the

◆

THIRTEENTH TALE

◆

MAUREEN BRANCALEONE

MINERVA PRESS
WASHINGTCN LONDON MONTREUX

TWELVE TALES OF GOOD WOMEN
AND THE THIRTEENTH TALE
Copyright © 1994 Maureen BrancaLeone

All Rights Reserved

No part of this book may be reproduced in any form,
by photocopying or by any electronic or mechanical means,
including information storage or retrieval systems,
without permission in writing from both the copyright owner
and the publisher of this book.

ISBN 1 85863 122 X

First Published 1994 by
MINERVA PRESS
2, Old Brompton Road,
London SW7 3DQ.

Printed in Great Britain by
Martins the Printers, Berwick upon Tweed

TWELVE TALES
of
GOOD WOMEN
and the
◆
THIRTEENTH TALE
◆

CONTENTS

PREFACE

A WORD OF EXPLANATION

These tales, which have been written over a period of years, are in a way the distillation of a lifetime of living as a foreigner who found herself integrated into a culture light years distant from the cold Celtic one into which she had been born. They appear only now because they have always taken second place to other, more 'important' work, but they have always been my closest friends. It gives me the shivers to re-read some of them while others, above all 'Mothers', gave me the shivers to write. But they were things that had happened, to others or to me, and eventually they had to come out. Italy, where many tales are set, is a country where black is blacker and white is whiter than anywhere else and so it lends itself to striking contrasts, at least to this eternal foreigner.

Why the title? What is so good about these women? I think that 'goodness' in this context emerges as a strong instinctive sense of justice coupled with an equally strong sense of purpose. Each one of the central characters from the unfortunate Gertrude to the even more unfortunate Ornella, Emma and Douce knows by instinct what it is she has to do and does it.

English readers will note the vital role played by respectability in the lives of these women. Perhaps this would not have been the case had they not been Italian. Eccentricity has never been truly understood or appreciated in Italy. Latins are very down-to-earth and fantasy is not for daily life. In fact dismayed parental protests were rife in the schools where Alice in Wonderland was adopted as a text book.

These good women belong to no social category. They are just simple, elemental women whose actions are directed by their instinct as well as by their brain. They have not moved all that far into civilisation. They can and do put up with accepted, conventional injustice but not with the more devastating injustice of Fate that the law can neither reach nor touch. That is the injustice they rebel against - a nose suddenly growing, being hated by the one you love, having your children unjustly taken from you. Even Mrs Brown with her outraged sense of decency and Miss Abegail with her innocent daring are rebels. Beatrix is the only one who flies away from it all. And she dies.

M.B. Rome
March 31st 1994

THE FIRST TALE

THE NOSE

THE NOSE

Gertrude was sure that her nose was growing bigger. Every time she looked in the mirror she studied it, and every time she became more certain that it occupied more space on her face, as you might say; it was changing shape, and not for the better.

What sinister mechanism could be at work inside her, Gertrude asked herself over and over again in the long sleepless nights which had become her lot since the discovery. Why does a nose, a perfectly normal nose, suddenly start to grow? Night after Gertrude went over all the possible causes she could think of - glandular imbalance, protein/vitamin intake, hormones - but she could never find a satisfactory solution to the problem; just the damned cussedness of her nose.

She could confide in no one, that was the worst of it. Indeed she shrank from formulating her problem in words, for in some instinctive way it seemed to her that if it were crystallised it would lose its private nature and become, if anything, even more menacing.

But then, she would argue with herself some nights, if I were to tell someone about it, to whom could I turn? Jilly, Selena, Nancy - her women friends were out of the question. She knew that although they would express concern, inwardly they would be laughing at her. And the news would spread like wildfire. No, women friends were out. Her mother? A stout sensible woman who gardened a great deal, her mother would dismiss the whole thing as one of Gertrude's 'fancies'. If pressed, she would become impatient and tell Gertrude that really she ought to be more grateful (to whom was left unspecified) instead of always worrying about her appearance; she would draw to Gertrude's attention to all the poor sick people in the world who had more to worry about than their noses, the spastics, the cripples, the thalidomide victims, not to mention lepers, whose noses were sure candidates for departure.

The only possible sympathetic person was Adrian, Gertrude's husband. And here she hesitated. A woman never does like to admit to her husband that she has some physical defect. Then, the possible outcome of such a confidence was two-fold. One, he might not have noticed in which case he would start noticing after she had told him, in the way men have; two, he might have noticed already and have deliberately refrained from saying anything to her about it, in case he should hurt her feelings. And in this latter event Gertrude would only be stupidly, tactlessly dragging out into the open something which her husband's innate delicacy had preferred to leave unsaid.

Which left her with no one, just no one at all.

You may think at this point that Gertrude worried excessively about her appearance, and this cannot be denied. Yet, paradoxically, she was not a vain woman. It was exactly because she was not vain that she worried. In a way the Gertrude who wrestled with the problem of her nose had created herself; out of a fat, plain adolescent she had dragged a slim and almost beautiful woman. Yes, Gertrude had worked on herself. Since she had disliked her reflection in the mirror at the age of fourteen she had set out to change it, and she had succeeded. But her eye had remained critical. Therefore it is true to say that she was not vain. Her aim was (if we may say this without being laughed at) philosophical: she wanted to appear as she had always felt herself to be. And now her nose was ruining the result of years of hard and painstaking labour.

Poor Gertrude! She had no children, because she had not chosen to have any; she had feared for her figure. She had a pleasant job and an easy, pleasant life and plenty of spare time in which to think. And so the problem of her nose came to assume, in a short time, such proportions to her that she began to avoid looking at herself in the mirror. She taught herself to avoid the one in the bathroom; it was quite easy, once you got used to it.

In the end she went through the ordeal of looking at herself once a day only, when she put on her make-up in the morning; apart from this occasion she kept her eyes averted when passing all mirrors.

Some nights she tried to be constructive, to think of all possible remedies. The most comforting, the most likely, it seemed to her, to help was of course plastic surgery. But immediately the objections arose in her mind. It was expensive. And what if the new nose started to grow too, afterwards? And in any case how could she manage it? Adrian hated the idea. Once when she had laughingly said to Jilly or Selena or Nancy in his presence that one day she'd have a facelift, Adrian had exploded, surprisingly, for he was a gentle man. "Don't you know what happens to people with facelifts?" he had shouted. Jilly or Selena or Nancy had been quite shocked. So unprogressive! "After some months their skin begins to droop again and they look worse than ever. Then they've got to have another one. You can't do anything about ageing skin except put up with it." Gertrude's skin was not exactly ageing, and she was annoyed with Adrian for implying that it was in front of other women, but in her heart of hearts she was not really offended. Indeed she found, on reflection, something comforting in Adrian's bluntness. It meant, in the last analysis, that he didn't mind, that his affection for her went deeper than skin deep, that he loved her for what she was, not what she looked like. But at the same time it meant that she would never be able to have a facelift without deeply offending Adrian - and this she didn't want to do - and the thought was depressing. It was like taking away the hope of eternity from a believer. Without a facelift what would she look like at sixty?

One night during this most anguished period, Gertrude walked in her sleep. In the morning, still in bed, she told Adrian about her strange dream. Adrian hated listening to people's dreams, but Gertrude always told him hers all the same. She had dreamt, she said, that she had got out of bed and had gone into the corridor where, on some bookshelves, stood a chiming clock. "I picked up the clock and let it fall deliberately" she said. "It made a terrible jangling noise, but no one woke up. Then I picked it up, put it back on the shelf and went back to bed".

Adrian, who had been listening absently while he knotted his tie, agreed that it was a very odd dream, and left for the office. Gertrude got up. On her way to the bathroom, as she passed the bookshelves, she glanced instinctively at the clock, and sudden horror gripped her when she saw that it was standing with its face to the wall.

That same evening, forcing nonchalance, she said to Adrian, "Oh, by the way, darling, the clock I dreamt that I dropped last night had its face to the wall this morning." Adrian couldn't remember much about Gertrude's dream, so he said vaguely "Oh, did it?" And Gertrude went on unsteadily, "That means that I didn't dream that I dropped it. I did drop it!"

After hearing her account of the dream once more and after having ascertained that the clock had really been dropped, for it could chime no longer, Adrian, somewhat disturbed, advised a visit to the doctor.

The doctor, a busy man, listened to the story of the clock impatiently and prescribed a light tranquilliser. He asked Gertrude if her sex life was quite normal, heard that it was, then told her that above all she was not to worry. The thought of her nose flashed into Gertrude's mind and for a split second she was on the point of telling the doctor about it, but then she saw that he wasn't listening anymore, indeed had already pressed the bell under his desk to summon the next patient, so she picked up her prescription and her handbag and left without saying anything.

She slept better with the light tranquilliser, yet although she no longer lay awake at nights thinking about her nose, that was not to say that the problem was solved. When she would wake up in the morning, after a night of dreamless sleep, the first depressing thought that crashed into her mind was... that.

Weeks passed, and Gertrude began to neglect her appearance. Shopping no longer interested her. She even gave up going to the hairdresser, in case they should notice. She began to do her hair herself, and she wasn't very good at it. When it lay flat on her head in the most unbecoming fashion, her nose seemed perfectly enormous and she could bear the sight of herself even less than before. She became moody and ill-tempered, refused to let Adrian come near her, and withdrew more and more into her tormented self.

It was during these bad weeks that she forgot, one night, to take her tranquilliser. She went to bed early, as she had taken to doing, and fell into a deep sleep. What happened that night is almost too terrible to relate.

All that Gertrude knew about it was that she was awakened by an agonising pain in her face. She opened her mouth and at once felt something warm and sticky pouring into it. Choking and retching, she tried to scream. Adrian leapt out of bed and switched the light on, to see Gertrude standing beside the bed with a pair of tailor's scissors in her hand and blood streaming from her nose. "Good God, Gertrude!" he exclaimed in horror. "Have you gone mad?" He rushed her into the bathroom, got cotton wool and surgical spirit and water and tried to clean her face of the blood and tears; then he told her it would hurt and poured surgical spirit over her poor nose which was horribly gashed by the scissors with which Gertrude, in her sleep, had tried to cut it off.

THE SECOND TALE

EMMA

EMMA

She was a little woman and she was faded - faded in the way only blondes fade when they age. Her hair, dry as straw and the same colour, was bunched up and held in place by a twisted scarf. She had boots on, and a fur coat, much worn. Her hands, red, rough and ringless save for the plain wedding band, clasped a cheap handbag. It was her face, though, that made the sergeant feel so uncomfortable. Expressionless, pale, with dry lined skin around colourless eyes which might once have been blue, a cigarette drooping from dry lips, it was the face of a person from whom all life had ebbed. Half an hour before the sergeant had listened to the incredible story; without really believing the woman he had still phoned through to the Commissioner and sent two men round to her address. He could not help thinking that the poor thing needed a doctor.

Later, the small crowd which had collected round the door of the police station stared, unbelieving too, at the little woman as she was pushed, not too roughly, out to the waiting van. The word had gone round - most people knew one another on the housing estate - and now they stared at her in silent horror. Men dropped their eyes, women drew their children closer to them. They could not understand. How could they understand? And yet, she had had her reasons for what she had done.

It had all started fifteen years before, shortly after her husband, a one-time partisan she had left her hill-farm home to marry, had left her for another woman. She had realised soon after her marriage that he was a layabout, a petty thief, so his desertion did not upset her as much as it might have done. She had been supporting him anyway, she had been in service and had then had the luck to get a good job in a small hand laundry; now she had only herself to feed. In the laundry she ironed with the steam iron for ten hours at a stretch; sometimes at the end of the day she felt as if her back would break, but she had the rent of her furnished room to pay and she never had been one for the easy life of whoring. She was fresh in those days, her eyes were blue and she was tall, with a full healthy figure.

She first saw Carlino in the laundry, one day during the lunch hour, when she was alone, since the owner and his wife went home to lunch; she was eating her bread and cheese when Carlino knocked at the door. He worked with the railways as a conductor on the night run up north and he needed his uniform pressed at once. It was the lunch hour and she didn't have to open the door to him, but he was handsome, and the face he made so appealing that she got up, opened the door, took his suit and pressed it for him with care. He thanked her and complimented her on her skill and said he'd come back for her next time he was down south. And sure enough two evenings later he was waiting outside the laundry door.

Within a month she was living with him, in the slum block apartment on the edge of town. He was good to her, but his old mother disliked her and did her best to make trouble between them. Emma did not get on with his sister either; however, as long as Carlino was there the two women had to take second place to her. Carlino was proud of her because she was blonde and tall, and people took her to be a foreigner. He liked to take her out; when he had a Sunday off they'd go up to the hills on his motor-cycle and make love and then go to one of the hill villages to eat a pizza and drink wine. She handed over half of her wages to the old woman for her food and board.

They had been living together for a year when she became pregnant for the first time. To tell the truth Emma could have avoided it; if it was anyone's fault it was hers, for Carlino was very careful. He had a horror of disease, and had caught a dose of the clap once, he told her, when he was in the army, and he never wanted to risk it again, so he took his precautions. When he heard she was pregnant he accused her of going with other men, but this was only by way of making it clear to her that he was no fool; he didn't believe it himself, he was sure of her. Anyway, the old woman would have known if she had been getting up to any tricks in his absence. He proposed getting rid of the child, but an abortion cost a lot of money and there was none too much to spare. So nothing was done, and the child grew undisturbed in Emma who was happy, feeling in an obscure way that it was a link between them, a step towards respectability and a home for just the two of them with no relatives getting under your feet in the kitchen.

As the months went by she had to give up the laundry, the steam iron was too heavy and the damp heat made her feel faint. now she had to stay at home with the old woman all day; it was hard, but she put up with it. Once the child was born, she thought, everything will change.

Nothing changed, of course, except that she had to get up at night to feed the baby when it cried and to keep it quiet on the nights Carlino was there. After a time, when she had partially weaned the baby, Emma went back to the laundry; Carlino made his old mother look after it, and they all got used to the little creature. Carlino actually became fond of it.

Two or three years passed without particular incident; Emma was still fresh and good-looking and Carlino was still fond of her. Emma thought her life wasn't at all bad, if it hadn't been for the old woman she would have been as happy as she knew how to be. On Sundays she and Carlino still went out on the motorcycle; they didn't make love on the hillside anymore, but they nearly always did when they got back home, a bit dizzy with new wine.

When she fell pregnant the second time something warned her to keep it a secret until it was too late to do anything about it. Abortion was not her only apprehension; two children to keep might seem too much to Carlino, and there was nothing to stop him from turning her out of the house. However, although he struck her when she finally had to tell him, and swore that she did it on purpose, and kept away from her when her body grew bloated and her face haggard, he did nothing. The old woman grumbled but by now Emma knew how to keep her in her place; she had discovered that the old woman lent money to her even poorer neighbours and took back in interest at least half of the capital. Carlino would have gone black with fury had he ever heard of this, for he cut quite a figure in the neighbourhood with his smart Wagon-lits uniform, and to be a usurer in Italy is worse than being a thief.

The second child was a girl, blonde like Emma. Carlino came back to her in time, though he threatened her that if she ever did it again he would leave her. Emma went back to her steam iron once more and when she got home at night was too tired to do more than eat and go to bed. The children hardly knew she was their mother, they saw so little of her; still, they grew up as so many others do and are none the worse for it.

All this time Emma had been saving, every penny she could keep back from her wages. Her goal was the apartment she had always dreamed of, modern, with a real bathroom with a door you could lock and a bath. In the slum block they lived in you had to wash in the kitchen, keeping an eye on the door, and the privy was cold, perched as it was in a corner of the narrow kitchen balcony.

One Sunday she persuaded Carlino to take her out of town, to what had once been countryside, to see the new apartment blocks going up there. They spent the whole day looking at apartments, big and small, and in every one Emma saw herself, mistress of her own home, presiding in her shining white kitchen which no cockroach would ever deface. She imagined the curtains she would put up, which would be the envy of the neighbours, the bedroom where all the fabrics would match, even the divan and easy chairs where she, for once a hostess, would entertain. Perhaps that Sunday was the happiest day of her life.

On the way home she told Carlino her secret; that she had enough money saved for them to put down six months' rent in advance and enough left over to buy some furniture - the kitchen and the bedroom, she said, the rest they could do in time.

The idea appealed to Carlino; when he was on duty on the train he felt important, he saw wealthy people who spent the equivalent of a week of his wages just to dine and sleep in first-class luxury on their way from one place to another. It humiliated him somewhat to have to come home to the slum block he had always lived in, to pass through the groups of dirty screaming children playing on the sidewalk, to let himself into the dank hall which always smelt of onions. A smart new apartment would be quite another thing; he thought that at last his private life would be more in keeping with his public one.

Emma would have dearly liked to get rid of the old mother, but alas, with her job in the laundry she needed the old woman to look after her children; she did insist, though, that Carlino marry her in church, a form of marriage which is not registered and is therefore not legally binding, but which made her feel a respectable woman.

Carlino agreed to everything, after some parleying; he knew that the marriage meant nothing to anyone except Emma, and he knew too that she still had a husband somewhere in the world, so that he was doubly safeguarded.

Some time after they moved to the new apartment Carlino met a pretty German girl on the train. She was on her way back to her home after a spell as a governess with a rich family. She reminded him of Emma as she had been when he first knew her, blonde and fresh and full. He fell in love with her and she, after the manner of German girls, asked no questions. She must have been at least fifteen years younger than Carlino, a point in her favour. She would come to the frontier station to meet him when his run of duty took him on that line; they would go to a little hotel. And sometimes Carlino stayed up there for his off-duty periods, phoning Emma to tell her that he had to put in some overtime. Emma noticed nothing at first; he was not quite so ready to make love, perhaps, when he came home, but she too was tired, for now she had a fairly long trip morning and evening by bus to the laundry, and when she got home at night she would set about scrubbing and washing clothes, however tired she was. The children had started going to school, she wore a wedding ring on her finger, the old woman was becoming too heavy to get around much and so was no longer a thorn in her side.

One day the old woman did not wake up in the morning; it didn't matter really because Emma always left the children's breakfast of milk and yesterday's bread ready for them, however, when she got home at night she found the two of them cowering outside the front door. When she burst into the old woman's room in a fury, it was to find her cold. She had been dead for at least twenty hours, the doctor said; Emma must call Carlino.

She knew the number up north where Carlino ought to have been; she dialled it and was told that he had been off duty for two days. They didn't know where he could be found, but they said they'd do their best. Emma was left feeling as if the roof had collapsed on her head. She had no doubt as to where Carlino was; he had another woman, she was sure of it.

He got home the next day, wept noisily over the corpse of his mother, had to be held down by his work-mates such were his transports of grief, and eventually fell asleep fully dressed. Emma said nothing. She meant to wait until after the funeral.

They were home, still dressed in black; Emma had had her cloth coat dyed at the laundry where she worked, for half price, Carlino wore a black tie and had a black crêpe band on the arm of his jacket. The children had not gone to the funeral, a neighbour had kept them. Emma did not know how to go about confronting him with her suspicions, so she did so clumsily, screaming at him in sudden rage. Carlino leapt to his feet as if he had been stung, gave her a slap that sent her staggering and left the house at once, banging the door so hard that it nearly came off its hinges. He had not even seen the children.

He came home again a month later. He wanted Emma to forgive him. It had been only a passing thing, he said, she knew well enough that he wouldn't play a dirty trick like that on her. There were the children, weren't there? and he had married her in church, hadn't he?

Emma agreed to forget it, after all he had married her in church and that was as good as... well, nearly as good as... and what man could be said to be faithful? She knew that they all did it the moment they got the chance. Some of her neighbours, with a houseful of children they didn't know how to feed, were even thankful that their husbands got it out of their system elsewhere. It was almost a sign of respectability.

What she didn't know was that the German girl had had Carlino's baby, and that the affair had been going on for nearly two years, and that she had had to leave home and that Carlino was paying the rent for her in the frontier town up north.

Years passed, the children grew up, Emma and Carlino quarrelled more and more frequently. Money was short and seemed to be getting shorter every day; Emma suspected Carlino of not giving her his fair share of the housekeeping money, and now and again she tackled him on the subject. Carlino took to coming home only once a month, then he began to skip months and sometimes they did not see him for as long as six months at a stretch. Emma was getting more and more tired; she would willingly have given up her job at the laundry, but she could not afford to, and besides, her wages had gone up and she did no more ironing except in an emergency. Now she was the supervisor, and had two girls under her. But the cost of living seemed to rise more steeply than anyone's wages increased, the children were always growing out of their clothes, and Emma prided herself on their appearance. Carlino liked to see them smartly dressed too, on the rare occasions he was around.

Perhaps it was the fact that Emma kept on at him about where the rest of his pay went to, perhaps the German girl bullied him into it, but whatever the reason, one day up north Carlino and the German girl went to the local town hall and got legally married. It must have been the German girl who made Carlino promise to tell Emma about it; left alone, he would never have had the courage. Anyway, one weekend in summer, he gave the children money to go to a movie, then sat down and threw his marriage certificate on the table in front of Emma.

For the second time Emma felt as if the roof had fallen in on her, only this time the floor had given way under her feet as well; stunned at first, she soon became hysterical and through her screams made for the kitchen where she grabbed a carving knife which she tried to use on him and then on herself, cutting her wrists for all she was worth. She was too excited to make a good job of it, though, just lost a lot of blood and had to be taken to the nearest hospital for first aid. Carlino didn't wait to hear the outcome; when her neighbour brought her back home later on he had gone.

Nothing could alter what was done, however, but what she could not admit was that her marriage with Carlino, in church, was the one that didn't count legally. And what did Carlino mean to do now? This was the question that throbbed in her brain, day and night. She tried ringing him up, but he was never to be found at the number he had given her. She could only wait until the next time he came home - if he ever did.

In the meantime, she bought a gun. What she bought it for, whom it was intended to be used on, she could not have told you. But she bought a gun, and hid it in her top drawer under her underclothes,

The gun lay in the drawer and Emma, some days, forgot that it was there. Other days she would take it out and practise with it, unloaded of course. She had put in quite a bit of practice by the time Carlino turned up again. He had come to have things out, he said, there was no use getting worked up, he was married now and Emma had better get used to the idea. He walked up and down the bedroom floor as he ranted and he did not notice that Emma had the gun in her hand until her silence disturbed him, and he looked at her, and there she was with a black shiny thing in her hand, looking at him in a kind of considering way. He turned ashen grey and dropped his pompous air, became almost grovelling. Emma was the only woman he had ever loved he told her, tears choking him, he had thought of a way out. They could emigrate to Australia and start a new life together. Wouldn't she like that? Emma, placated, put away the gun; she did not completely believe him but it was pleasant to pretend to herself that she did, that she was loved, and the thought of a new life was a beautiful one to play with.

Later that evening she moved the gun, in case he should think of taking it. She hid it under the bath.

They made love that night, and Carlino was ardent as he had not been for a very long time. Perhaps the sight of the gun had excited him. Perhaps he was frightened for his life. In any case, when he left the next morning Emma was happier than she had been for many months. A few days afterwards she telephoned him. Although she knew that he was of course living with his wife up north, this need for communication with him formed part of her new happiness. She had gone to the Australian consulate, had made enquiries, discovered that she could manage to pay the special immigrant fare. A woman's voice answered the phone, a hard foreign voice with a guttural accent. After some minutes Carlino came on to the line. His voice was belligerent. Emma paid no attention, started to tell him about her enquiries, the cost of the fare, all that she had found out at the consulate. He cut her short, brutally. It was no use, he said, it was over, he hated the sight of her, she made him sick, didn't she ever look in the mirror? Now that he was married, properly married, she had to learn to leave him alone. Did she think he was going to leave his legal wife for her? Why, she was no better than a prostitute! She might as well start thinking of getting out of the apartment - her apartment! - for he was going to come down one of these days and collect the children - her children! - and take them up north where they would have a respectable home with a respectable woman to look after them.

Emma put down the receiver. He had not finished his tirade yet she had no need to listen any further. All of a sudden it had become quite clear to her just why she had bought the revolver. He could take away everything else - the years they had been together, the apartment she loved so dearly - but he could not take away her children. She would not let him.

She made her preparations methodically. She put the loaded revolver into the pocket of her apron, the one that hung in the kitchen; she set the table, prepared the children's lunch, and sat down to wait for their homecoming. The girl got home first, jubilant with the news that she had had good marks at school that morning, then she seized a roll of bread from the table and sat down with it, pulling the bread hungrily apart and mechanically putting the pieces in her mouth, her eyes fixed on the comic open in front of her. Emma suddenly bent forward and kissed her on the cheek, an unusual gesture for her; the child, surprised, looked up, smiled at her, then looked down again and went on with her reading. Perhaps the moment was now, Emma thought; the child was perfectly happy. Softly she drew the gun from her apron pocket, steadied her finger on the trigger and pressed it. not once, but two or three times. The child never raised her eyes. She just fell forward on the table, a dark hole in the centre of her forehead and another in her neck, the half-eaten roll of bread still in her hand soaking up the blood that flowed down her arm.

When Emma heard the second ring at the doorbell she got up slowly. The gun in her pocket was still warm. She opened the door and kissed the boy standing there, who looked at her in surprise. Then he rubbed his cheek against hers, as if to let her know that he was happy. Soon he will have to shave, she thought, he is getting to be quite a man. When he turned to put down his books Emma swiftly raised the gun to the level of his neck. He too fell forward in a heap; the hole in his neck was bigger than Emma expected, but she had been very close to him. A gash of bright red blood stained the clean white shirt she had ironed for him that very morning.

Now it was done. Emma did not touch either of the bodies. She had performed her duty; let others do the rest. Carlino would never now take her children away from her. She went into the bathroom and washed her hands and put on some lipstick; in the bedroom she looked out the old fur coat Carlino had once found in an empty sleeping car - it was a very cold day - then she checked her keys, and pulled the front door shut behind her.

He can't have everything his way, can he? she thought exultantly. Still, I'd better let them know at the police station. Emma had always been a respectable woman, who liked to have everything in order.

THE THIRD TALE

ORNELLA

ORNELLA

"So he's dead! Died at last. Well!"

Oh, it happened a long time ago, must be over twenty years now. Yes, right in this very town. I was a young married woman with small children then, and so was she. We met through my husband who was at that time one of the team of surgeons in her father-in-law's nursing home. Her husband, Guido, was a doctor there too. We became friendly, if you could call our relationship friendship; I was sorry for her and she confided in me. In a way, the outcome of it - of what I am going to tell you - is nothing more than conjecture on my part, but that kind of conjecture which you know in your inmost being to be right, absolutely right.

Her name was Ornella and she was unhappy, I could see that straight away, the very first time I met her, when Piero and I went to pay our respects on Christmas Day. Yes, here in Italy they still set store by such courtesy visits. You take flowers, maybe, or a plant, and stay about half an hour.

They all lived together in a big house with several floors attached to the nursing home - the old professor and his wife, two unmarried sons, both students of medicine, and the eldest son Guido, Ornella's husband. They had got married while he was still a student - there was some story about that too - she was a country girl from some mountain village and all the town talked, there being such a difference in their backgrounds. The old professor had a country-wide reputation and his family was socially the first in town. Some people said that it was his father who forced Guido to marry Ornella, since he had got her pregnant and the old professor was very severe, an absolute dictator to his family. Anyway the first child was born six or seven months after Ornella's marriage, so there may have been something in the gossip.

That Christmas Day I found the atmosphere somewhat stifling. The old man and his wife and Guido and Ornella and their three children were sitting stiffly in the grand drawing room, receiving visitors. Maids were coming and going with flowers and plants and trays of liqueurs and sweet biscuits; and there they were, like so many potted plants themselves, sitting on stiff gilt chairs, the old woman dressed in some rich black material, Ornella badly dressed, without make-up, as if she didn't care. Guido paid no attention to her whatever, as if she weren't there; he seemed bored and only brightened up when Piero came in. The two of them were quite friendly and were much of an age. I was left on my own so I sat down beside Ornella. She was very shy and looked at me, a foreigner, much as if I had been some kind of exotic beast at the zoo; but then I asked her about her children and she became a little more animated. Before we left I had got her to admit that she sometimes went out, indeed took her children every afternoon to the Delfini Gardens. When I said that we lived near there it was she who suggested us meeting.

On the way home I questioned Piero pretty closely about the Ornella-Guido set-up. He laughed at my curiosity but he did say that yes, Guido did not seem very well matched with his wife and that he had had several extramarital adventures that most people knew about. "Don't mention anything to her, though, if you meet her" he warned me, and I promised that of course I wouldn't.

A few days later I saw Ornella sitting on a bench in the Delfini Gardens, knitting. Her three children were playing so I sent my own two to join them and sat down beside her. It was not long before we were talking about our respective lives, and she wondered how I found life in Italy as a married woman. I said that I was perfectly happy, which was the truth, and she sighed. I asked her if she was not happy and she said oh yes, of course she was, only that living with her in-laws was depressing. She didn't feel as if she was in her own house - as indeed she wasn't, I thought - her mother-in-law was a bit of a tyrant, there was never a chance of being alone with her husband, although as far as being alone was concerned... She stopped, and got up abruptly, called her children and said good-bye to me. I was left feeling rather cheated.

Somehow she preyed on my mind. I could not stop thinking about her. One day I suggested to Piero that we invite Ornella and Guido for dinner, just the four of us. Piero at first objected that we did not really know them well enough to invite them to an intimate dinner, however when I insisted, pointing out that I was doing it because I wanted to help Ornella, he gave way.

The dinner party cannot be said to have been a success. The insufferable Guido - for to my mind he was already insufferable -

arrived with his wife and from that point on seemed as if he were entirely on his own. He never looked at her; never referred to her, never spoke to her. I did my best as a hostess to link up this strange couple, to draw out Ornella, sitting silent and mortified, to make Guido talk about her if not to her. It was no use. Guido paid compliments to me, joked and talked shop with Piero, then on the subject of our little town waxed very bitter. He had had enough of the provinces, he said, he couldn't stand much more of it, the gossip, the dullness, the lack of entertainment. This seemed to provide me with a good opportunity to ask Ornella what she thought of her husband's opinion, but Guido swept aside my query with the remark "My wife doesn't agree with me, of course. She's a real provincial."

When they left I felt miserable, as one does when a party has been a failure. Piero said nothing about the evening, and I did not feel disposed to starting an argument, for as men always do, he would probably have taken Guido's part and I by this time felt so strongly about Ornella that I would certainly have made an issue of it.

We did not meet in the gardens for some time after that disastrous evening and then one day Ornella appeared with her children. She sat down beside me, more awkward than usual. She seemed to be trying to tell me something. At last she said "I'm sorry about the evening. You know, when we came to you for dinner. I'm sorry if I spoilt the party."

The words were out before I could stop them:

"You! But if anyone spoilt the party it was your husband!"

And then I said "Oh!" and could have cut my tongue out. One does not criticise the husbands of acquaintances, even of good friends, to their faces. Wives may say all sorts of things about them, but let no one else agree, far less attempt to make a remark that even hints at criticism, or they will be hostile at once, up in arms, fiercely defending.

Ornella, however, said nothing. She bit her lip and then: "You mustn't mind him. He's always like that with me. It's an old story. I know you meant to be kind in inviting us, but now you have seen for yourself - we just don't form a couple, or rather, he doesn't form a couple with me. He can't stand me, and he doesn't care who sees it."

Bluntly and baldly, it was out. Conscious of my gaffe, I tried to laugh off her last remark.

"Oh, we all say that or something like it, when we've had a quarrel."

She turned great dark tormented eyes on me.

"But we haven't had a quarrel" she said slowly. "Or rather, our whole married life has been one long quarrel."

"Oh" I said, and started to fumble for a cigarette in my bag. Automatically I offered her one, but she shook her head. She seemed to have gained confidence.

"You see" she said, "I am a country girl. He is the son of a famous doctor. He used to come up to my village in the mountains, where my parents are both school-teachers, to ski, and one winter he started to court me. He seemed like something from another world to me - I fell in love with him. He would take me dancing, take me out in his car, and one night I let him - we made love in the back seat of his car. I loved him - I still love him - and I was, I suppose, attracted by the idea of change, another life, the city, getting away from the village. And then I found I was expecting his baby. I hadn't heard from him since he left - perhaps for him the story was finished - and I wouldn't have made a fuss, but my mother found out about it, and she and my father wrote to his father the professor. They're very respectable, you know. They couldn't have borne the shame if Guido hadn't married me. The professor came up to our village and questioned me. Then he told me not to worry, he would see to everything, he was satisfied that I was telling the truth. And, in fact, the week afterwards Guido wrote a formal letter to my parents asking if he could marry me. I know, of course, and I knew even then that he had not written spontaneously, that his father had forced him to do it. But then I thought that once the baby was born everything would be fine - and I loved him, and when you love someone the way I loved Guido you can't believe that they don't love you. It's impossible to believe. So we were married. The very first night of our honeymoon Guido began to treat me as he does now, openly, in the restaurant, eating as if he were alone, never even looking at me, and then afterwards in the bedroom he flew into a terrible temper. He said he would never forgive me, that I had ruined his life, that I had blackmailed him into marrying me, that I had gone to his father knowing that the old man would have forced him to marry any slut of a girl - that is what he said, I shall never forget it - that happened to conceive a child by him. He talked a lot about men and their needs and how many children they could sire in their lifetime and love having nothing to do with it."

She stopped, and covered her face for a moment. Then she sighed, a great deep sigh, and went on.

"And since then, over all these years, that has been our relationship. Every now and then he would become so angry with me that he practically raped me - that is why I have three children, whom he professes to love."

This appalling tale was told quietly, without tears and without drama. I was petrified.

"But then" she took up her story once more, as though talking to herself, "He fell in love with a girl, and everything was worse than before. It started about two years ago. She is a nurse in the nursing home, blonde and tall, and he loves her. He loves her!"

Here she really broke down and wept, twisting her handkerchief in her fingers as if out of that damp piece of cotton she could extract some comfort.

"From the start I knew he had someone. You know that we live in his parents' house. So that if he doesn't come home at night they notice. Well, I had to cover up for him! Yes, even that. He was often away for nights on end, and he would tell me what to say. I had no choice. I had to cover up for him while he made love to his girl friend. But this year it has been getting worse. Sometimes he seems to be mad. I have had to phone her more than once, to tell her how pleased I am that he has found a companion. I have had to ask her pardon for standing in the way. I have had to thank her for her... for her..."

"And couldn't you have?..." I was out of my depth. "I could have told the old professor, asked to be allowed to go home. But think of my parents, the shame of it! And in any case, you see, bad as it has been, bad as it is - I'm bound to him in some way. No, I can't leave him."

"Well, I don't know". I got up. I felt I had had enough for one afternoon. My cool English blood revolted at the spectacle of this woman, humiliated beyond measure, resigned to her humiliation, so enchained by the ties of family, conventional ties and more - and this was the worst of it - emotionally bound to her torturer.

"If I can help you in any way..." I looked at her, trying to think how I could help her.

"No". She got up, collecting her things. "No one can help me. Only I can help myself - if I can find the courage."

And with this she left me.

Days and weeks passed and Ornella never came to the gardens. I asked Piero about her and he said he thought she had gone to her parents for a rest. She had not been at all well, indeed seemed to be on the verge of a breakdown.

"I don't wonder" I could not help saying. Piero looked at me closely.

"What do you know about her?" he asked me. I shook my head. Piero's job at the nursing home was important to both of us and there was no point in involving him in this story which, after all, had nothing to do with either of us. Why I felt so deeply about it I don't know. But Ornella was after all a sister woman, and what had happened to her might have happened to me.

The summer holidays took us away from the town. We spent a month all together by the sea, then Piero went back to work and I remained at the sea with the children. When we came home it was October. Piero told me one day that Ornella was back in town, but that she was confined to bed, and would very much like to see me. The message had been given him by one of the maids.

Of course I went, that very afternoon. The atmosphere of the house seemed not to have changed at all since Christmas, I was shown into the drawing-room before going up to see Ornella, and there her mother-in-law was waiting for me. The old lady did not seem unkind, but on the other hand she did not display any affection for her daughter-in-law, of whom she spoke as if of a rather troublesome child.

"It's very good of you to come" she said graciously. "There's nothing really wrong, of course, but Ornella has never been strong you know, not at all the ideal wife for a doctor. I don't know what she would have done if she'd had to live on her own with her husband. She could never have managed a household. All she has to do here is look after her children and even that seems to tire her. She has just come back from the mountains, we thought it would do her good. But no, nothing seems to do her good. Nothing organically wrong with her, nothing at all. Just weakness. So my husband has ordered her complete rest in bed and a course of liver injections to put her back on her feet".

When I was shown into the big, gloomy bedroom I was shocked at the change in Ornella. She had always, since I had known her, been pale and thin, but now the face on the pillow seemed a tiny white smudge devoured by her dark eyes, which seemed enormous, and the arms lying on the coverlet were positively skeletal. Tears came to my eyes as I bent to kiss her.

"Ornella" I said. "What have you been doing to yourself?"

"I don't know, I can't seem to keep on my feet" she said, smiling faintly. "Yet my parents fed me like a prize turkey. In the mountains I was better".

"And Guido?" I asked her. She turned her face away.

"Guido?" she said listlessly. "Oh yes, he comes in every night to give me my injection. Apart from that I hardly see him. He's often away. He tells his father he has patients in the city. At least I don't have to phone his girlfriend. He suggested that she should give me my injections - can you imagine that? But my father-in-law put his foot down. He said that since they contain liver extract they suppurate easily, and it is better if they are given by a doctor."

I sat down, not knowing what to say.

"Well, now you will feel better" I ventured at last. "There's nothing like liver extract for bucking one up."

She looked at me. "I think I'm dying" she said slowly. Then she stretched out a bony hand. 'If anything should happen to me will you keep an eye on the children?" she asked humbly. "Just a friendly eye - they're all so fond of you. You know, they call you their English aunt." "Do they?" I said, thinking the while, poor little things, if they are left with that father! And, very shortly, with that step-mother. "But you're not going to die, Ornella, you mustn't die if only for the children's sake. You're going to get strong and healthy, and then you must take a decision - you can't go on living like this."

"That's true" she said, "I can't go on living like this. I've been reading a lot lately' she went on inconsequently, "Mainly detective stories. They interest me, and I forget for a little while. In this one I've just finished a husband gets his wife to kill him - oh, she doesn't know it of course - because he knows he's dying of cancer and he knows too that she has a lover. So he saves up his sleeping pills and grinds them into a powder and when he's got enough he puts the powder into the glass of medicine which she brings him every night.

He knows that they'll say she poisoned him, and there's the motive of the lover, so she'll get a life sentence, and that is his revenge."

"Ornella, what a horrible story! " I laughed, aloud. "I'll bring you something a bit more cheerful to read - that sort of thing is not for a sick person. What about some trashy love stories?"

She looked at me steadily. I realised that again I had made a gaffe.

"Love stories, no" she said. "I can't bear them." It may have been my imagination, but I thought there was a wildish glint in her eyes.

"But don't you think it was clever?" she persisted. "You see it's the perfect crime, if you can call it a crime to get someone to kill you when you're dying already and when above all you know that they desire nothing better than to get you out of the way. No one but the wife ever gave him his medicine, and no one would ever believe that he wanted her to kill him so that she would be punished for it. If she was not guilty of killing him she was guilty of wanting to kill him and all he did was to enable her to do what she wanted. It's too fantastic!"

She seemed really carried away by this rather horrific story, and I wanted to get her mind off such subjects, so I began to tell her with an enthusiasm I was far from feeling about our children, their school marks and sayings, and even launched into the field of new clothes.

"When you get up we'll go on a shopping expedition to Florence" I said. "I am dying for something smart to wear, but I'll wait until you are better. And we'll go to a beauty parlour and have a treatment, and buy some new make-up. You'll see what fun it will be!"

She smiled wanly. Obviously clothes and make-up did not interest her in the least. I thought it was time to leave since I could see that talking and listening tired her.

"Wouldn't you like some more light in the room?" I asked her before I left. "Shall I open the shutters a little? It's such a perfect October day." And indeed the afternoon sunshine had turned to burnished gold the leaves of the great plane tree beneath her window. She shook her head. "The light hurts my eyes" was all she said. So I left.

I looked out some books for her and gave them to Piero the next day. And then, a few days later, we went to Bologna together, since

Piero had a patient there and I wanted a change of scenery. I still love days out with my husband, lunch in a restaurant, just the two of us, then wandering round doing some shopping perhaps, or sightseeing. We got back late at night pretty tired, and went straight to bed. In the middle of the night the telephone rang. It was the nursing home. Piero got dressed in two minutes, and was out of the house in five. He didn't come back until morning, and when he did he looked haggard and somehow older.

"Well, what was it this time?" I asked him. I was still in bed.

"It is - or was - your friend Ornella" he said slowly. "She's dead."

"What?" I leapt out of bed and seized my dressing gown. "How, dead? Dead of what? She can't be dead - I saw her only a few days ago. They said there was nothing really wrong with her." My heart was beating crazily and my hands were trembling.

"Something very unpleasant. The professor has accused Guido of killing her. The injection - you know she had an injection every night - well, the one he gave her last night did not contain liver extract, but a massive dose of digitalis - to simulate a heart attack, you know. It must have killed her at once. Somebody switched the phial. And yet... it must have been Guido, it couldn't have been anyone else; Ornella herself prepared the injection every night, she liked doing it, it was something for her to do. She boiled the syringe on a little gas burner they had in their room for coffee and so on, then she left everything ready on a tray - the sterilised syringe and the needle, the surgical spirit, the cotton wool. No one else ever did this. Only Ornella. So it must have been Guido! He must have been crazy, though. He must have known it would come out. Of course he had phials of all sorts of medicines in his bathroom, mostly commercial samples, a whole arsenal of them. And yet, the strange thing is that he denies it - he actually denies it! The broken phial was lying there on the tray, for anyone to see. His father accused him at once. There was some scene there last night, I can tell you. I thought they had all gone mad, I never saw anything like it. The old mother in her dressing gown with her hair in a plait down her back was screaming at her husband - he must be mad, she screamed, how could he accuse his son, his own son, of a thing like that, and for a slut of a girl, that is what she said, those were her very words, for a slut of a girl you would accuse your own son! Never thought she felt like that about Ornella. I still hear the sound of her screaming, and the sobbing...

sobbing for Guido, not Ornella. Poor Ornella, she was still warm, but she was dead, I certified it myself."

"And how" I struggled for speech, "how did they discover?"

"He gave her the injection and went out again. To that girl, you know, I suppose. She dragged herself to the door of the bedroom and tried to call for help. The old couple heard her and rushed to her. They sleep on the same floor. Then they called for me. But she was already dead when I got there. The old man had thought it was a heart attack - that is what it looked like - but when I went into the bedroom I looked at the broken phial. There were a few drops of the liquid still in it - I've sent it round to the lab - but there's no doubt about it, it was digitalis. As soon as I showed the old professor the phial he changed colour. "I didn't know it was as bad as that" he said. "My God, he has killed her, he has killed her." And then he phoned the police. Guido only came in about two hours afterwards. Of course the fact that he wasn't there, at that time of night, made his position even worse. He hasn't a leg to stand on."

Piero stopped talking. He looked very, very tired.

"I'll go and have a shave and a shower" he said. "It's a horrible business."

I sat down on the bed, my head in a whirl. 1 was too shocked even to weep. I was certain, yes positively certain, that Ornella had done the thing herself. She had wanted to die or rather, it must have seemed the only way out to her - since she knew that she would never, never bring herself to leave him. She loved him, she had insisted on that when she was telling me her story, she loved him and therefore she couldn't leave him. And yet she could not go on living with him... the detective story she had told me about must have given her the idea. She shared the bathroom with her husband and all the medicines were there. She had only to take her choice. A doctor's wife doesn't make silly mistakes between digitalis and liver extract. She knew what she was doing, of course.

No, of course, I didn't tell anyone my suspicions. Only I knew about the detective story. Why should I have spoilt Ornella's revenge? And if anyone deserved to expiate, it was Guido. He killed her morally and physically. She started dying the day she married him, but really dying, of a disease as pitiless as cancer. He gave her cancer of the spirit, if you like. He had no pity. Why should I have had pity on him?

He died the other day in prison, still protesting his innocence. He suffered too, you know. Lost all his hair and his teeth, contracted some nervous disease. Twenty years it took to kill him. Ornella's revenge was great, it is true, but then so was her love. Great.

THE FOURTH TALE

DOUCE

DOUCE

She had been christened Annalise, but her mother called her Douce, because she was such a sweet baby with big, trusting dark eyes and a little hand that would pat your shoulder comfortingly when you took her in your arms. The name stuck to her during her childhood and, subsequently, all through her life.

She was an only child, the last and only one of the eight or nine her mother had conceived to see the light of day. She was therefore very precious to her parents, well-off and respected citizens of the little southern town in which they lived. Her father was the local doctor, who painted sea-scapes when he was not on his rounds, her mother the daughter of the notary. Nothing was too good for Douce; a little pony cart for her to drive when she was small, the best convent school when she was older, her clothes ordered from the best shops of the capital.

Both her mother and her father expected her to marry well; apart from her affectionate, generous nature, she was attractive with her dark eyes, long curling hair and mobile, expressive mouth. And since she was an only child and the town thought her father to be wealthy, suitors were not lacking - but Douce liked none of them,

One Christmas she was invited by an aunt by marriage who had relations in Austria to spend the holiday with her in Kitzbühl. Douce's parents were delighted, for this might prove to be the chance of a lifetime, and so was Douce, for she had never yet seen snow, nor indeed been far from her home town. In Kitzbühl she met a young Austrian called Wilhelm, blond and cold, with piercing blue eyes which had a hypnotic effect on her. Without quite realising it, Douce fell deeply in love with him, which was what the young man had intended her to do, for her aunt had let it be known that she was quite a catch. Wilhelm surrounded her with his highly civilised attentions, and when Douce returned home she was what is known as unofficially engaged.

Wilhelm did not let much time elapse before introducing himself to Douce's family. In all probability he wanted to inspect them for himself. He came to Sicily on a visit, well-dressed, well-mannered and possessed of a steely charm. All the ladies of local society were quite captivated with him, Douce's father, the doctor, was not completely convinced but since his wife was enthusiastic and since for years he had taken his cue from her, he made no serious objection to having Wilhelm as a son-in-law. After all, Wilhelm's mother was a baroness and although the young man had not yet started to earn money, he had a law degree and had prospects of joining a firm of solicitors in Vienna.

They became engaged, as is the custom in the south, with a ceremony which in grandeur fell little short of marriage. Wilhelm gave Douce one of his mother's rings, a huge diamond coupled with a black pearl. Douce was delighted with it, more on account of size than taste, her mother, who saw an evil omen in the colour of the pearl, a little less, however, they were engaged and the marriage fixed for the following year.

"A year at least" Douce's father stipulated. "So that Wilhelm will be earning by the time you are married. After that, if children come..."

Douce was at that time eighteen. A child of the south, she could not be said to be ignorant of sexual matters, but they had no concrete reality for her, for she was by nature innocent. Thus when Wilhelm, on one of his visits, found her on a hot afternoon curled in a chair in the living room, half asleep - it was the siesta hour - and, moved despite himself, took the opportunity of initiating her into womanhood, Douce hardly knew what was happening to her. She did at first protest somewhat feebly, but Wilhelm's caressing hands soon put a stop to that and very soon she was oblivious to everything except the hard male body crushing her, piercing her, and finally pleasing her. Before the siesta hour was over Douce was a woman and she loved Wilhelm for what he had done to her.

About two months after Wilhelm's departure, unfortunately, Douce's father began to notice that his daughter's looks were fading; her face had grown thin and pale, her eyes were listless, her appetite had disappeared. Unwilling to harbour perhaps unfounded suspicions, he did all the same call Douce into his study and question her closely. Douce was too honest and she loved her father too much to lie with success. The doctor learned that one of the greatest misfortunes a man can suffer in the south had befallen him; that night he had a heart attack and they had barely time to send for the priest. In the morning Douce was fatherless.

The shock was a terrible one for both mother and daughter, but when the doctor's affairs were gone into the disaster assumed even greater proportions. For years they had been living above their income; in the goodness of his heart the doctor had cured most of his patients for nothing, accepting only payment in kind, a chicken perhaps, or a couple of bottles of good wine. He had also been - perhaps in the hope of setting things right - a heavy gambler, and they discovered that all the property was mortgaged to pay the debts he had incurred at the card table. Even the house they lived in no longer belonged to them. All they had left was the clothes on their backs and the furniture which belonged to Douce's mother.

"At least you have Wilhelm," Douce's mother exclaimed through her tears. "Thank God my darling at least you will have a husband to look after you."

"And you will come to live with us, mother." replied Douce hugging her. "You will see, things will turn out all right in the end. God always provides."

Wilhelm sent his condolences. Some short lime elapsed, and then two letters arrived; one for Douce's mother, in which he explained that since her daughter's circumstances were now greatly altered, and since he himself could boast of no personal fortune - his widowed mother the baroness was in control of the family money - he could do nothing except beg leave to break off the engagement. It was a beautifully written letter, and extremely courteous. Douce received a letter too, in which Wilhelm professed himself to be deeply distressed but unable to foresee any future for them as a couple. His mother had absolutely forbidden the marriage, he wrote, and, as Douce knew, he was still entirely dependent on her for money. He was kind enough to add that Douce might regard the ring he had given her as her personal property. There was no need to return it.

Douce was a girl of character, and she behaved well in a crisis. It was the first real crisis in her life, which had, until recent months, been such a sheltered one. At this point some girls might have thought of suicide, but Douce thought of her mother, bewildered and distraught, and she thought of the child in her womb whose existence had killed her father. And if she wept often and bitterly, it was when she was alone in her room and it was not out of self-pity. Obscurely she felt that she was caught up in some ancient and inevitable cycle of crime and punishment, and that all that had happened she had somehow deserved. Wilhelm's desertion seemed to her almost just. Had she not killed her father?

"For after all" she said to herself, "it wasn't his fault. He couldn't go against his mother."

She would have liked to keep the ring, but she felt it would not have been fair. So she put it in a little box and sent it off by registered post. Then she tried, but did not succeed in composing a suitable letter.

Douce's mother almost went out of her mind. She could not understand what, all of a sudden, had happened to them, and she could not contemplate a life which must, of necessity, be very different from that she had lived for forty years. What would become of them? Sitting all day in her shuttered room, dressed in her widow's weeds with a long black shawl over her head and shoulders, she was a tragic figure. And yet she did not yet know the full extent of the tragedy. Douce was very conscious of this fact and was very brave and very tender with her, almost as if her mother were a hurt child and she its comforter.

And all the time she was thinking, always thinking. At night she would lie awake, adding up their resources, working out plan after plan. One thing was certain, they would have to go to live somewhere far away. She could not expose her mother to the spite of the local gossips. She went to see the parish priest who sent her to the nuns. The Mother Superior, after hearing the story, suggested moving to the city. She would write, she said, to the sister house there and Douce would find the nuns helpful. Nuns can be very helpful indeed, if they want to be so.

Douce sold some of their furniture and organised their departure. Her mother let her do everything without protest. She only asked if the move was really necessary and when Douce replied that it was, she said no more.

They found a small flat in a new, poorish district in the city and Douce found work as a night nurse for old, bedridden people whose relatives could afford to pay others to look after them. It was not a pleasant job. It meant very little sleep at night, for the old people slept fitfully and every time they woke up would ask for something, a glass of water, bedpan, their pillow turned. Douce was thankful to have it, though, for it was difficult for a girl like herself, with an excellent education but no diplomas, to get any kind of paid work.

She and her mother had just enough money to pay the rent, something over to buy food, and no money whatever for extras. Douce walked to work to save on fares. However, her mother had always been an excellent needle-woman and, again through the nuns, she got work embroidering priests' vestments for several parishes. What with little sleep and little food, Douce lost weight instead of gaining it, so that even her mother did not notice any change in her until she had reached the seventh month.

Douce had never found the courage to tell her mother and the poor woman took the news badly. Coming as she did from a family in which respectability was prized above every other virtue, she could not forgive, indeed could not understand her daughter. For the first time in her life she hated Douce - no better than a street-walker, no wonder Wilhelm had left her, thank God her poor father had not lived to see this day! Now what were they going to do with a baby on top of everything else?

Douce listened in silence. There was really nothing for her to say. Her mother was right, she felt, she had really behaved very badly; how could Wilhelm possibly have married her after what she had done? The strange thing was that although she knew that she must be guilty, she did not feel sinful, and this lack of conscious guilt seemed to her the proof of her depravity. When her mother had worn herself out Douce helped her to undress, put her to bed and gave her a sleeping pill, then she lay down on the bed beside her trying to think things out.

Her pains started that night and she had to drag herself out of bed and go to knock at a neighbour's door to ask them to call an ambulance. After a long and agonising labour a baby girl was born, tiny for she was a seven months' baby but perfect in every way.

She called the baby Natalya after Tolstoy's heroine. She had always loved Russian literature. There was no formal baptism since they had baptised the child as soon as it was born in case it should not live. After some weeks Douce took it home and put it on to a bottle. Her life was a hard one but she never complained. Now that she had work and a roof of her own and a bed of her own she felt that she was lucky. Also she was too busy to repine. She had to keep on putting up a brave front for her mother's sake, for if Douce accepted her destiny with courage the same could not be said of her mother. Once of a cheerful disposition, the older woman had became bitter and resentful. She was often angry with Douce who had spoiled their lives, she said; at other times she would weep silently and this was harder to bear. Her hair, which had once been brown, was now quite white, and her erect figure had become curved with leaning over her embroidery. Her beautiful eyes had faded and she had to wear spectacles. When Douce got home in the mornings she was very tired, but the first thing she did was to buy the milk and make breakfast for her mother and her daughter. After this she would go to bed.

As Natalya grew up and passed insensibly from the state of baby to that of toddler to that of little girl, she became if possible ever dearer to Douce who had lost so much through her. Sometimes she would crush the child to her in such an access of passion that the little one would cry out in pain. Her grandmother too adored Natalya and it was she who dressed her, copying the prettiest clothes from the magazines. Natalya had blond curls, liquid dark eyes and smooth pale olive skin. Her beauty was so unusual that people would stop in the street to admire her. And as she grew up she showed that she had also a very strong will. Douce and her mother spoiled her, of course, and never went against her. So that by the time Natalya was five, she ruled the little household completely.

When she was six she had to start school and it was a sad day, all the sadder because Douce had to leave the space on the entrance form blank where normally the father's name would have appeared. Perhaps this more than anything else brought home to Douce the fact that her child was fatherless.

Perhaps Douce over-compensated for this and certainly Natalya lacked for nothing. At Christmas her toys were more numerous than those of many a richer child, and her clothes were always beautiful even if made at home. No one at school or elsewhere could imagine the effort that all this cost her mother.

Years passed and Douce, strange to say, had no lovers. Perhaps it was not so strange for such was her struggle to live and keep alive those who depended on her that she had neither the time nor the energy, above all she had no love to spare. That is until she met George.

He was a young man, some years younger than she when they first met. He was the grandson of an old Colonel she was nursing, and one morning he happened to be there when she was leaving the house.

He was fair, like Wilhelm, but he had kindly eyes and a gentle mouth, unlike his predecessor, and when he saw Douce, pale and exhausted after her night's work, he felt sorry for her and attracted by her. He was at the beginning of a journalistic career, and he thought that her story must be interesting. So he took to being around when he knew she would be coming off duty, and he would often give her a lift home in his car.

Douce's mother began to notice, and she began to worry. The neighbours would talk, she said, and did Douce want to start causing trouble again, now, when at last they were getting along not too badly? And what about Natalya? Had Douce thought about her daughter? For by now the grandmother loved her grandchild more than she did her daughter.

Natalya was then ten years old. She was exceptionally bright at school, and the leader of her class in everything. Study cost her very little effort, and she was beautiful. At home she would help, if she felt like it, otherwise she would shut herself up in the bedroom with a book. She could spend hours and hours by herself, lying on the bed listening to records on the record player her mother had bought her on credit. Sometimes Douce worried about her, and wondered what was in the child's head, and hoped that she would turn out well; but then she would think again that Natalya was a good girl at heart and that if she was silent and withdrawn sometimes it was probably due to her age.

After some time George began to suggest meals together, trips on Sundays, and Douce, after a little struggle, began to accept these meetings. After so many years of real hardship it was good to feel wanted, to have someone who was interested in her and what she thought. Little by little she told George her story, without ever mentioning the name of Natalya's father.

One night when she was free, for now and again she had a free night, George and she became lovers. They had had dinner in a pleasant restaurant in town, which had taken Douce back many years to before, and then George had driven them to the beach. It had been a hot summer's day, and the full August moon was just beginning to rise, blood red, paling as it climbed. George told Douce how much he loved her and that she was making his life unendurable; he could think of nothing but her, he said, his work was suffering. Surely she understood him? Douce let go at last and murmured yes, but he must be careful please; she was not quite so innocent this time as she had been before. George took her very gently at first, lying on the soft sand, still warm from the day's sun; then he took her again and again and Douce, for the first time in her life, knew what real pleasure was. She lost all sense of time and place; her only reality was the dark blue sky, the now coldly brilliant moon, the soft plash of the waves and the man making himself part of her. Memories stirred, sometimes; but her encounter with Wilhelm had been too fleeting to leave any lasting impression.

After that they would meet every night that Douce was off duty. They took to going to George's little flat, and Douce would leave, softly so as not to disturb him, in the early morning.

One day the old Colonel died and Douce found herself out of a job. It had not been her only job but it had been the one that paid best. The Colonel had been her only 'regular'.

George, seeing her worried, suggested that she and Natalya move in with him. He offered too to pay the rent for her mother. He could well afford this for he had inherited all his grandfather's money.

This was Douce's opportunity; she should have refused and held out for marriage. For George would have married her with very little persuasion. Douce however never dared speak of marriage, thinking of her past and the years that separated them, and so she never said anything and George let things go. After all there was time, there was plenty of time.

Douce and Natalya moved in with George despite the fact that her mother grumbled. However Douce brought her gifts of food, bottles of wine, things she had not been able to afford before and the old woman had reached the stage where all she asked of life was comfort.

Douce was happy. She loved George, with the visceral love a woman has for her love-child, or her first lover. George too loved her. Better living, and above all love, had filled out her pale cheeks and given back sparkling life to her deep-set eyes. She was sweet-tempered, always happy, a good cook and an efficient housekeeper. And she was a passionate lover. In the jungle of the city no one asked for a marriage certificate and soon she was known in the shops around as George's wife. She went often to see her mother and thanked God for the turn her destiny had taken.

Natalya was not so pleased at the turn of events. She was more silent and withdrawn than ever and she seemed to resent Douce's happiness. Perhaps, having always had Douce to herself, she was jealous of George. She was barely polite to him and always managed to have something to do when he was at home. George tried to win her over with presents, but these she would leave pointedly unopened or, if pressed to open them, aside. On the rare occasions that the three of them were together Douce often caught George looking at Natalya, as if he were trying to discover her secret.

After a few months of this uneasy life George suggested sending Natalya to boarding school. He thought, he said, that she would be happier. She was too much alone.

Natalya did not want to go to boarding school, and she did not want to leave her mother. She wept long and bitterly when Douce told her that she had found a school and then she did something that she had never done before. She turned on Douce with spite and hatred. She was vicious, wanting to hurt. Douce was sending her away, she stormed, because she was jealous of her. She was jealous because she was afraid for George. She, Natalya, was young, and George liked young women, even if he didn't know it. Douce was getting rid of her, that was what it boiled down to. But she would have her revenge, she swore. However long it took, she would have her revenge,

Douce, listening to these accusations, thought she must be going mad. Her head swimming, her eyes brimming with tears, she tried to approach Natalya, to take the child in her arms, to tell her how absurd her suspicions were. But Natalya would not let herself be touched, covered her ears and would not listen to her. She locked herself into her room, and it was in sullen silence that she left some time later for boarding school. Douce tried to make conversation during the car journey but Natalya would not respond. Locked in sullen silence she stared out of the window all the way, and when they left her at school she allowed her mother to kiss her on the cheek and even to hug her desperately, but she remained totally unmoved. As they turned to wave to her they saw her already walking away.

George did his best to comfort Douce in the weeks that followed. He told her, over and over again, that it must have been a shock for the child, that Natalya was over-possessive with her mother since she had never known a father. He told her that it was natural for a child in shock to turn against those she loved best since she felt that they had betrayed her. Douce allowed herself to be comforted, indeed for days and weeks on end she let herself slip into a kind of somnambulistic state during which she really believed that nothing had changed, that Natalya loved her again, that everything was as it had been before.

George by now had to travel often and when he was in the vicinity he never failed to pay a visit to Natalya. Douce was grateful to him for this, it was yet another proof of his devotion to her and his real kindness of heart.

Natalya came home for her first holidays and if anything, she had grown even more beautiful. Not for her the agonies of adolescence, spots and puppy fat. She was tall and slender, yet not thin, her movements were graceful, her hair the colour of ripe corn and her dark eyes, usually watchful, could be in turn yielding and compelling. She behaved as if nothing had ever happened between herself and her mother, but so polished was the performance that Douce's heart bled when they were together.

She returned to school without fuss and George said to Douce that his cure was working. "You see, she's quite all right again" he said, and Douce agreed yes it really did seem as though Natalya were quite all right again.

* * *

NATALYA'S DIARY

Monday, 1st October

This is my first day at a boarding school. I hate it. They brought me here yesterday by car. Mother was all soppy. No, she wasn't soppy, she was really upset. But I didn't let her see I minded, not one bit. I hate her for agreeing with George. They wanted to get me out of the way, that's all. Do they really think I am so stupid? Just because now she lives with George must I be pushed out?

They'll see I can't be got rid of so easily. They'll see.

Tuesday, 2nd October

I am going to write the story of my life. Everybody in my class must write the story of their lives. Mine will be the most exciting. I have got a special copybook for stories. Mother Joanna wants us to write lots of stories. Mine will start like this:

My name is Natalya and I was born to a beautiful lady ten and a half years ago. Like the Baby Jesus I had no father, we have never seen him so I suppose he does not exist. I lived with my mother and my grandmother until six months ago. when my mother went to live with a man called George who said I must come too. Now they have had enough of me and they have sent me to boarding school.

Friday, 5th October

They have taken away my copybook with my story. I was writing it during recreation yesterday when an older girl whose name is Margaret came up and asked me what I was doing. I showed her my story and she took it to the nun in charge. They did not give me back my copybook. Oh God oh God please let me go back to mother! Let George disappear! Why can't we go back to living as we did before, with grandmother?

Sunday, 7th October

Reverend Mother called me. I was rather afraid. I went up to her little room where she sits at a desk. She smiled at me and told me to sit down. She asked me why I had written what I did in the copybook. I said because Mother Joanna told us all to write the story of our lives. I said that was the story of my life only I couldn't write any more because Margaret took away my copybook. I said, please had I written

something wrong? Reverend Mother said no, you have
not written anything wrong. It is just that sometimes
people don't understand. And she gave me back my
copybook and told me to come and see her whenever I
liked. I like Reverend Mother.

15th January

This is the first day after the Christmas holidays. I
stopped writing my diary because I got bored. But I
still think that I will keep a diary, if people won't read
it. At least I can say what I think in it. Now I am
going to talk about the Christmas holidays. First I
must describe my mother and George.

My mother is small and dark and pretty. She
loves George. George is a man who writes articles in
newspapers. He is tall and fair and good looking.
Mother loves him very much. I think that George also
loves mother. Neither of them pays much attention to
me. Mother used to love only me, before she met
George. When they brought me to school last October
I had been wicked. I got into a rage and shouted things
at mother and she cried. Now I am not in a rage any
more but I still think they don't want me. One of these
days I am going to write the story of my life and tell
the truth about everyone! Now I have not enough time.
This Christmas was not too bad. George and mother
bought me lots of presents, even a little typewriter,
there was a Christmas tree and a crib. On Christmas
Eve there was a lovely supper, cold turkey and
mayonnaise and potato salad and ham and they grilled
sausages over the fire and then there was a big cake
with cream on it.

On Christmas Day we went to see grandmother.
She was grumbly as usual, and cried when she saw me.
I couldn't cry back. She gave me a present too. It was
a writing case, with writing paper and envelopes and a
little pocket for stamps and a place to keep your pen

and pencil. I have not been wicked any more. I kissed
mother and let her kiss me but I still haven't forgiven
her. It was better without George.

George and Mother took me to the circus. I think I
am a bit big for that sort of thing. I made up my face
one day for fun with mother's make up, and George
got very cross with me. My little poppies are starting
to grow. Mother says in a few months I shall need a
bra. Uffà! I started having what mother calls my
periods just before the holidays ended and came back
two days late. Have I to put up with that all my life?
Mother says you get used to it. I don't think I ever
will.

15th February

George came to see me last Sunday. He brought
me a big box of chocolates and some books. I had to
give the books to Mother Joanna. She will give them
back to me when she's looked at them. George said
they are very interesting books which have been
translated from English. One is called David
Copperfield and another The Golden Days. George
kissed me good-bye and told me to be good and said
had I any message for mother. I said no. He said the
books were for my birthday. Tomorrow I shall be
eleven.

16th February

Today is my birthday. It's not as nice having it at
school as at home even if the other girls are all nice to
you and the teachers don't give you any bad marks.
Mother sent me a parcel and there was a cake in it and
little packets of sweets and some money. I can't spend
the money until the holidays unless I buy black babies,
but I don't think I'll buy any black babies because you

never see them. They stay in Africa. Now I am feeling very sad. I hate the dormitory, all white and all the curtains drawn and the big light in the middle that dazzles your eyes when you are in bed until they put it out and after that you can't read any more. Only I can read because I've got a torch but I have to read under the covers because if they find it they'll take it away. I have even got a spare battery. I think I'll write to George and ask him to bring me two more if he comes see me again.

15th March

George came to see me again. He brought the batteries. He took me out and we had a lovely afternoon. We went to the biggest shops in town and bought lots of things, even for Mother.

1st May

The Easter holidays were quite fun. Mother bought me a bra. We went to see my grandmother. She started quarrelling with mother straight away over my clothes. She says I shouldn't be allowed to wear trousers. I went into the bedroom and read magazines while they were talking. Grandmother gave me a glass of marsala.

I AM NOT GOING TO KEEP A DIARY ANY MORE. THE GIRL IN THE CUBICLE NEXT TO MINE HAS BEEN READING MINE ALL THE TIME. I FLEW AT HER AND BIT HER WHEN I WENT UP TO THE DORMITORY TO GET A HANDKERCHIEF AND FOUND HER AT IT. HORRID PIG!

* * *

Some years later Natalya came home for the Christmas holidays and Douce's mother fell ill. She had been living alone all this time, although Douce had always paid her frequent visits. As time passed these visits became more and more painful to Douce, because her mother seemed to be growing to hate her. Complaints, veiled criticisms, reproaches were the order of the day, and Douce got to the point where she had to screw up her courage even to ring the familiar doorbell. Yet when one night a neighbour of her mother's phoned to tell her that the old lady had been taken ill, she felt cold and stricken. Her mother was going to die. The last link with the past was about to be broken. She got dressed quickly and called a taxi.

Her mother lay ill for quite some time, and Douce moved in with her and nursed her devotedly. She had had a heart attack, the doctor said she might recover. Everything depended on how Douce nursed her. After a few days she seemed to rally, and then Douce was faced with the problem of what to do with her if she got better, for she felt she could hardly ask George to take her. However, she did not get better. Her kidneys began to fail; her blood pressure, which had been high, fell steadily. Douce, who had nursed so many old people, knew what was happening. It was the end.

At four o'clock one February morning she died. Douce, who had been sitting up with her, had fallen into a doze. She was wakened by a kind of gargling sound and instinctively stretched her arms to her mother, who was staring at her with terrified eyes. Her tears fell on the dying woman's face, and rolled down the withered cheeks which were still wet when death came. Douce dried them carefully afterwards.

She phoned home to tell them what had happened, and soon after George arrived, with Natalya. The undertaker came in later, and George and Natalya took Douce home.

In the days that followed Douce was too exhausted to notice a kind of complicity between her lover and her daughter. But one day some time after the funeral she came into the kitchen just as George and Natalya were sitting down to breakfast. This time she noticed the look that passed between them, and for the first time realised that Natalya wore nothing under her dressing gown, which was open down to her waist. She said nothing, however, but turned and went back to the little room where she had been sleeping alone since her mother's death.

No one could have done more for Douce than Natalya in the weeks that followed. Her boarding school was forgotten. She ran the house, did the shopping and cooking and even the cleaning. George came and went and Douce lay in bed and dreamed of her childhood with her loving father and mother, and refused to look reality in the face.

The time came though when reality was suddenly there, before her eyes, and she looked at it as if it were a picture. Months had passed since her mother had died; Douce had lain in her little room dreaming; Natalya had taken over and Douce had not tried to resist her. Not yet forty, Douce felt an old woman. Everything and everyone had left her; her father had gone from her first, then her mother and daughter, one might say hand in hand; George had gone from her imperceptibly, and she found herself quite, quite alone. She took stock of all these truths one morning early, and was surprised to find that she did not even mind. All her youth, and with it all her passion, had left her. And then, thought Douce objectively, it was true that Natalya had taken George from her, but Natalya was her daughter. So it was as if, in a way, Natalya had secured George for Douce. Without being married to him and older than he was, she could never have held him. One day he would have left her for a younger woman anyway. And this being a fact of life, who better than Natalya?

For the rest of her life, thought Douce, she could live near him, and look at him, and talk to him, and serve him. She could go on loving him, in a word, and he would know it and remember. George and Natalya would marry, of that Douce was certain. And she would look after their children, and it would be as if they were her own.

Douce got up resolutely, bathed and dressed with care, and then walked out of her room, the little room which would from now on always be hers, past the bedroom where George and Natalya were sleeping, to the kitchen.

She was going to make the breakfast.

Epilogue

Maternal love had triumphed in Douce or just love. She had given in without a fight, or perhaps she had not even realised that there was one. Perhaps she was just one of the losers, who are winners in the end because they have never felt like losers. Perhaps she had simply accepted.

She, Natalya and George lived under the same roof for almost twenty years. During this period George and Natalya married and had two children. Douce supervised the household and kept in the background, both things which she did rather well. Natalya got herself a job since she found that she was somewhat superfluous at home. No one ever mentioned the past, but Douce always said 'we' when talking about the family. As might have been predicted, George was perfectly happy with a very beautiful wife to look after and a wife-mother to look after him. Natalya was still moody and her old rancours were not altogether forgotten despite the obvious fact that she had won. Perhaps she felt guilty, perhaps she begrudged her mother the years she had spent as George's lover - who knows. Perhaps she could not or dare not look into her heart for fear of what she might find there. She had loved George fiercely and she had won him. Douce had loved him tenderly and she had lost him. But they had both loved him. Deeply.

When George died of a heart attack he was mourned by two women. He was lucky.

THE FIFTH TALE

THE NOVEL TO END ALL NOVELS

THE NOVEL TO END ALL NOVELS

Sturgis, the publisher's reader, hadn't had such a "good 'un" as he termed it, for years. There was everything in that novel; not a page but spoke of rape, fornication in all the positions, incest - all possible combinations of it - bloody violence, and most of the least commonly known types of perversion. Sturgis had become hot under the collar straight away, at chapter one, and had become so filled with lustful desires that he couldn't stay in the office any longer. He was afraid that he might attack one of the secretaries, and then where would he be? For nights after the event he couldn't sleep properly, for his dreams had become so turgid, and so erotic, that he kept on waking up to find himself panting, bathed in sweat, and when he fell asleep again it was only to dream some more.

"The Naked Brunch's nothing to it" he cried out unexpectedly in the local A. B. C. one day over his hamburger, and in the bus he was heard muttering about the absolute in pornography. He carolled in his bath, and he sat on his treasure. At last a find, a true winner, all gold, pure gold, just the thing to set the firm back on its feet. And he, Sturgis, had discovered it. What nonsense they talked when they said that people didn't read any more! Of course people read, more than ever what with telly being so permissive; there was no sense of sin left, thought Sturgis, that's what it was, and with the sense of sin had departed all the fun in sinning. That was why people read pornography, the type of book which gave them the illusion of actually sinning, of being right down there in the mud, sinning. And he, Sturgis, had found the book for the market!

At the end-of-the-month Editorial Meeting Sturgis drew out the manuscript from the pile in front of him.

"It's great" he announced, "It's the tops. The Naked Brunch's nothing to it" he concluded.

Strained silence followed his remark. The Editorial Meeting was pretty wary of works described as "great" since they used the term themselves on the blurb of particularly unsaleable novels.

"You mean, Mr Sturgis," said the Chief, Editorial Staff, precisely, carefully placing the tips of the fingers of one hand against the tips of the fingers of the other, "You mean that you have something *worthwhile* there?"

He smiled as if he had just uttered the most outrageous witticism, and looked round at the other staff members, who tittered obligingly.

"Well" said Sturgis undaunted, "I think you must judge for yourself, Mr Beeswick."

And he handed over the manuscript.

The next morning Mr Beeswick turned up at the Office looking positively haggard. He had been reading half of the night and his eyes were swollen and watery. The whole thing had also come as a shock to him. He sent at once for Sturgis.

"I hope, Mr Sturgis" he said as Sturgis carefully seated himself, "I hope you realise that what we have here is a bomb?"

Sturgis nodded eagerly, but Mr Beeswick forestalled him.

"This must be taken up at the highest level" he admonished. "The very highest. Of course it's a seller, but our policy has always been... and then there's the risk of prosecution. You do realise, Mr Sturgis, all the risks involved? I must implore you therefore to say nothing to anyone about this... this... this manuscript" he finished somewhat lamely.

Sturgis promised, and the manuscript went up to the highest level, to the office of Mr Dewlap, the owner of the firm, himself.

Mr Dewlap was still young, he liked a bit of hard porn, and unlike Mr Beeswick, he was immediately enthusiastic. Like Sturgis, he could see just how much fresh blood, to use a much worn metaphor, in terms of hard cash the "Kingdom of the Damned" would inject into the old publishing house which had been founded, in the early nineteenth century, by his great-great-grandfather "In order to further the teaching of Christ and aid in the spreading of Holy Writ". "Nonsense, nonsense" he said to Mr Beeswick's objections. "If they ban it, just think of the publicity! We'll publish in Paris, and all the left wing will raise an uproar, and the Archbishop of Canterbury will preach about "Damned" from the pulpit, saying that in content it can be compared to none other than Holy Writ itself! Oh, Beeswick, we're on to a good thing now!"

And Mr Dewlap rubbed his hands and went off to have a lobster lunch at the Savoy.

So a letter was written to the author, who strangely enough was a lady, in not too enthusiastic terms in case she should catch on to the importance of what she had written to the wilting firm of Dewlap and Dewlap, but inviting her to come up to town and have a talk with Mr Dewlap himself. The lady's name, again strangely enough, was Miss Abegail McPherson.

*

Miss Abegail McPherson descended from the taxi cautiously, and carefully transferred the money she had ready - for she always checked the meter on the rare occasions that she took a taxi - to the contemptuous palm of the taxi driver. This was Number Two Beecham Square, the holy of holies, the sanctum of Dewlap and Dewlap itself. She then mounted the well-worn steps, pushed open the black-painted door and entered the premises. A doorman in uniform requested her business and she told him that she had come for an interview with Mr Dewlap himself. The doorman let her go up, somewhat doubtfully, then settled back with the latest racing news, trying to pick out tomorrow's winners, a task at which he was an old hand, if not a great success.

The svelte, somewhat intimidating secretary asked Miss Abegail twice what her business was, then, having grasped that she was the author of "Damned" showed her in with an awed expression, after communicating her presence to Mr Dewlap, to the office of the great man himself.

Miss Abegail, smiling nervously, holding her mock leather handbag in both hands clasped across her chest as if in defence, took the necessary steps across the carpet to Mr Dewlap's desk. Mr Dewlap, standing, wore on his face an expression of pure astonishment.

Miss Abegail, if anything more ill at ease than he, said shyly, "You wrote to me about the manuscript, Mr Dew... Mr Dew... ?"

"Lap" snapped the publisher.

He could not rid himself of an inexplicable and unfathomable and in any case quite irrational dislike of his name.

"Yes yes yes" he said, trying to collect himself. "Please do sit down" he invited. "Have a cigarette... you don't smoke, Miss

McPherson? Just one minute, then, if you will excuse me for a second I'll be with you straight away."

He dashed out of his office, faced the astonished secretary, sent for the Chief Editor and Sturgis, obtained the fated manuscript, and returned to his desk.

"We think it might just have a chance" he began, once his collaborators were around him. "So - taking a big risk, mind you - a very big risk, however risk not want not - how is it the saying goes? In any case we have decided to take that risk. There may not, of course, be a very large profit in it either for the firm or for you. "

He eyed the little lady sitting on the other side of his vast desk with what he hoped was a suitably terrifying look. A full-length portrait of his grandfather - his great-great-grandfather had not approved of such frivolities - hung behind his desk, and he hoped he was behaving as the tradition of his house demanded. The Dewlaps had always been keen business men.

The little lady sighed, and smoothed down her dark grey serge skirt.

"As far as I am concerned, I don't want to publish for profit" was her amazing statement.

The three men leaned forward as if in concert, unable to believe their ears.

"No, not for profit" she said. "Money isn't everything. Some might call it vanity, Mr Dew... Mr Dew..."

"Lap" supplied the publisher, less irritably this time. "Thank you" she smiled at him gratefully. "Mr Dewlap", Mr Dewlap, Mr Dewlap... there! I've got it now. Now, as I was saying, some might call it vanity, but I sent you the manuscript in the hope that... well, in the hope that future generations might remember my family name. One has such a short time to live" she went on appealingly, "And, as Ezechial says - what does he say? I can't quite remember, however, it doesn't matter. We have such a short time to live, and then, what then?" she asked challengingly.

The three men nodded solemnly.

"So that it seemed to me" and she smiled as if to apologise, "That since I have a great deal of time on my hands, and since I have always been an excellent letter-writer" she smiled once again, "That I might leave my mark - my family's mark - on the world in some way, in this way, in fact."

She stopped.

There was a lcng silence.

"My dear Miss McPherson" Mr Dewlap was the first to recover himself. "My dear Miss McPherson" he went on warmly. "We are certainly, indeed most certainly, going to do business. "And don't think you're going to get away without a contract!" He wagged his finger at her, suddenly light-headed.

*

Miss Abegail McPherson, sitting in a second-class compartment in the Victoria - Brighton train, pondered. It had turned out to be a success after all. How glad she was that she had not only discovered, but sent up her poor brother Willy's manuscript to town! What a pleasure for poor dear Willy, now on the other side alas! of the
Pearly Gates! It had come as quite a surprise to her, the discovery that poor Willy had been a writer as well as a minister. You could almost say that it had come as a shock, for it did not seem quite the thing for a minister of the Church of Scotland to write novels, and that was why Miss Abegail had sent in the manuscript under her own name. Yes, yes she knew that people were so much more broad-minded these days, still there was a certain something connected with novel-writing, and if poor dear Willy had never tried to get it published... There Miss Abegail decidedly parted company with her late, beloved brother's views. It is true that in the Psalms vanity is severely condemned. But is the desire of the writer to have his work see the light of day vanity?

Miss Abegail did not think so, no indeed she did not most decidedly think so, and for this reason she had sent poor Willy's manuscript to the most respectable publisher she could think of, Dewlap, yes that was it, Dewlap who so many years ago had printed her late father's sermons.

Miss Abegail never read novels, and she had gone no further than the title page of Willy's, but she had no doubt but that poor dear Willy had written a good one.

THE SIXTH TALE

THE GREEK CALENDAR

THE GREEK CALENDAR

Mrs Brown didn't like the calendar at all. Not one little bit. Of course she could see that it was great art, admire the composition and all that - she wasn't an uneducated woman - but still, she thought privately, antiquity isn't everything, and just because a work of art belongs to B.C. everyone raves about it and if it had been painted or sculpted or written in this century it would have been labelled - quite rightly - as obscene.

That was what was wrong with the Greek calendar - it was obscene. Mrs Brown was no prude, of course, but she had her limits. Obscenity was one thing she could not take. Of course all parts of the human body have been fashioned by the hand of God, but still some should be covered. Even the animals have hair, don't they?

Mr Brown, an art dealer, had brought home the calendar in some triumph. Printed on the finest of paper, every month was illustrated by a "true" colour reproduction of Greek amphore, all of which had been photographed in the various museums throughout the world where they are to be found. Mr Brown had been very enthusiastic about the calendar. As he pointed out to Mrs Brown, it was quite something to have all that beauty under one's eyes in such a work-a-day place as the kitchen. Mrs Brown had agreed with him politely, as she usually did, since it was so much easier. Next day, however, when she was about to hang the calendar on the nail which the previous year had borne the missionary calendar of the Overseas Fathers, dedicated to the conversion of the Pagan, she had paused to look at the illustrations. January was all right. A Greek charioteer, side view, fortunately hidden by his shield. February - well, February would just pass. But March! In March four warriors of the Corinthian period - so the small type told her - marched across the best paper quite naked and with no attempt to conceal the fact. Mrs Brown pursed her lips. "This sort of thing won't do at all" she thought aloud, "Certainly not for the kitchen." And June! March, well March might get by, but June was really too much. A runner of the sixth century before Christ was running for all he was worth, all limbs extended to the full, and not only his limbs. But it was positively revolting! And what a very peculiar shape! Mrs Brown had not seen many male generative organs - well, she had seen her husband's, involuntarily of course, and she had two sons - but she had not had, shall we say, wide experience in that field. And the shape of these Greek organs were certainly very strange.

Mrs Brown hung up the calendar in the kitchen, since after all January was all right, and anyway where else could she have hung it up? In her drawing room? Not to be thought of. In her bedroom? Never! If, on the other hand, she did not hang it at all, her husband would ask her why, and then he would laugh at her, and tell her what a silly provincial woman she was and didn't she know that these amphore were masterpieces of early Greek art?

Mrs Brown did not like being laughed at for her "limits" as she called them. On the whole she liked to think that she was pretty liberal in her ideas.

Mrs Brown's sons were out in the world on their own and she and her husband lived alone in a smartish flat and she had a fair amount of spare time on her hands, "worrying time" as she called it. She was a worrier, and now she had something really knotty to worry about. The whole of January and February she worried about the coming of March. She could hardly look the daily woman Maria in the face in March. Maria, however, had never so much as glanced at the calendar, and indeed, if she had, she would probably never for a moment have connected the reproductions with living men. Maria was innocent of education and everything printed was, literally, a closed book to her.

As March ended and April and May went by, the Greek calendar became more and more of an obsession with Mrs Brown. At nights she lay awake, wondering what to do about the little red man scheduled to appear in June. If the background had been black, she reasoned, as in most of the other reproductions, she could simply have inked out the offending organ. But the background was a whitish cream colour. A piece of sticking plaster would look ridiculous. Cream-coloured paint likewise.

On the very last night of May, Mrs Brown had her brain wave. It was such a simple solution, so obvious did it appear to her, that she could not understand why she had not thought of it before. She would castrate the little man with a pair of scissors. Then she would turn over the little square of paper she had cut out and paste it back in place, with the white side uppermost.

Since there was no time to be lost she got up at once, quietly so as not to waken her husband, and slipped into the kitchen. She took down the calendar and laid it on the table, and then she looked in the odds and ends drawer for the kitchen scissors, and then, her heart beating loudly, she cut out the little square of paper. Now for the paste, and the job was done. Since it was June already, for it was three o'clock in the morning, she hung the calendar back on its nail and admired her work. There was something missing, that was true, but still it wasn't noticeable unless you looked very closely and no one really does look closely at the pictures on a calendar, what they look closely at is the date. Mrs Brown went back to bed and fell at once into a deep, sound sleep.

In the morning she got up, as usual, a little after Mr Brown and went into the kitchen to squeeze oranges and heat the coffee while he shaved. She was a trifle sleepy, so she didn't even glance at the calendar. It was her husband, coming into the kitchen freshly shaved in his pyjamas, who startled her by his exclamation. "Why, this little chap has changed somehow since last I saw him" he said, going over to the calendar to look closely at the reproduction. Mrs Brown turned round, looked, and fell in a dead faint on the red-tiled floor.

The chaste little square of white paper was there no longer, and the little chap, still running for all his might with all his limbs extended, now sported a perfectly monstrous organ completely out of proportion with the size of the little chap himself. There was a twinkle, too, in his painted eye that had not been there before. He gave the impression, if one could say such a thing about a sixth century B.C. painting, of being alive and of enjoying the situation.

THE SEVENTH TALE

THE WHITE CANARY

THE WHITE CANARY

Beatrix had gone to sleep under the big flowering chestnut tree on the edge of the lawn. She had been reading a book of poetry but the afternoon was hot and she had become drowsy and had drifted insensibly into unconsciousness. In her sleep she dreamed of greenness - the greenness that was around her and above her - and it seemed to her that she was not on the ground at all, but perched on a branch among the leaves.

When she awoke the sun had gone down and she was surprised to find that somehow or other she had indeed got on to the branch of the tree. With some terror she measured the distance that separated her from solid earth, and then she prepared to jump. To her astonishment she flew, for her arms had become wings, and her whole body was covered with the softest, downiest white plumage. She had turned into a bird.

Beatrix had always been a little person, with thin arms and legs and a sharp little nose and a way of holding her head cocked on one side when she was listening to anyone talking which had earned her, both at home and at school, the nickname of "Birdie". She had never expected, though, that bird indeed she would become one day.

She flew instinctively towards her home, the old long red house that dominated the lawn and yet seemed to be nestling among the tall trees where the rooks lived and from which their cawing could be heard so loudly, especially in spring. She flew past the drawing-room windows and saw her mother seated inside, her head bent over her needlework; she flew higher, and perched on the schoolroom window ledge, and saw her brothers at their homework. One of the children looked up and raised the cry: a white canary! A white canary! All the children flocked to the window and Beatrix, frightened, flew away and down in one great swoop that took her to the open kitchen door. She flew in, swooped round the familiar table several times, then came to rest on the back of one of the chairs. Then, with much noise and tumult, her brothers tumbled into the kitchen. Beatrix, frightened again, took to the air and escaped through the open door to the garden.

All that late afternoon Beatrix flew around her home, longing to enter and yet afraid, for she realised that she had become a very small and unprotected creature and that fear was now part of her nature. Yet as evening fell and the shadows lengthened she became even more afraid of staying outside among the animals and other birds who might not recognise her as one of themselves. So she flew back towards the house and perched just outside the kitchen door.

The children had spent their study hour in trying to catch her but had eventually given up and gone trooping upstairs. They had left as bait, however, on the table, the painted birdcage with their yellow canary in it. From outside Beatrix could see the yellow canary and as time passed she began to see safety in that cage. She hopped over the threshold, flew around the cage, perched on the table: the yellow canary chirped and Beatrix chirped back. Just then a hand closed over her, gently, and Beatrix was popped deftly into the cage.

Apart from the excitement of finding a white canary, there was considerable upset in the family that night, for Beatrix, the only daughter, was missing. No one could remember seeing her since lunch time, and her mother wept and her father called the police and there was talk of kidnapping. And all the time Beatrix chirped and gurgled as loudly as she could in order to attract their attention. If they would just look closely at her, she thought desperately, if they would just look right into her eyes, they would surely recognise her. But no one paid any attention to her chirping in the fuss and eventually, exhausted, she put her head under her wing and went to sleep.

The other canary was a male and he was very jealous of his rights. Beatrix had to wait until he had finished with the bath water before she could get near it. Otherwise he pecked her. It was some time before anyone in the family noticed this since the whole family was in mourning over Beatrix, but when her mother saw how cruel the male canary was to Beatrix she bought a new cage and put Beatrix into it, all by herself. Held for a fleeting moment in the maternal hand, Beatrix, her little heart pounding, hoped with all the intensity her little body was capable of feeling that her mother would recognise her and put off her mourning. But she hoped in vain, and indeed how could her mother ever have recognised her daughter Beatrix in a white canary?

Everyone said she was quite beautiful, and her origins were a mystery, and the children made up stories about her. Everyone said too how odd it was that the white canary should have appeared for the first time on the day that poor Beatrix had disappeared.

A year went by and Beatrix had almost forgotten her previous existence. I would like to be able to record that she sang her anguish, that the exquisite, despairing notes of her song filled the whole house with an indefinable sense of uneasiness. Alas, this cannot be recorded if we are to be truthful, for, as everyone knows, female canaries cannot sing. Beatrix chirped, and chirped as loudly and as tunefully as she could, but she cannot be said to have sung.

Another summer came, and the cages were put outside every morning, high on the wall, out of the reach of cats. Beatrix liked being outside; the sunshine made her happy, and the green of the trees brought back to her disquieting memories, she did not know of what. With her bath, and her fresh seed, and her little swing she was a most contented canary.

One day the children were preparing for an expedition to the sea, and their nurse reminded them that the canaries must be brought inside before they left home. They said yes of course nanny, but then they rushed about collecting bathing suits and towels and visiting the kitchen to see if their picnic was ready, and, in the end, when Beatrix heard the carriage wheels crunching over the gravel, she knew they had forgotten her.

She had no intimation of disaster, though. She had her bath with great pleasure, washing her snow-white feathers with pride, and she ate her breakfast and it was only then that she noticed that they had left her no drinking water. Some water did remain from her bath, to be sure, but Beatrix was fastidious and then there was so very little. The sun got hotter and hotter, and the children had also, in their excitement, forgotten to leave the roof of the cage covered, so that by noon Beatrix felt quite limp and exhausted and had not the energy to chirp. As the hot afternoon went slowly past she lay down on the bottom of her cage seeking protection, but even there there was no shade. Even her bath water had dried up by this time.

When the children came home in the evening someone remembered the canaries. They all rushed outside and a cry of distress was raised. The white canary was lying on its back stiffly, with its little absurd stick-like legs in the air. It was dead. The yellow canary was in bad shape too, but since its cage had been covered, it was still alive.

The children blamed themselves bitterly, and no one punished them for their negligence. Everyone thought that they had been punished enough by their loss. They then began to discuss the funeral. They did not want to put the beautiful white canary into the earth, where worms and other insects would defile it. So they decided on cremation. They made a little pyre under the flowering chestnut tree and placed the white canary, wrapped in several layers of cottonwool and strong brown paper, on it. Then they lit a match to the pyre and the little pile of dry sticks caught fire and blazed merrily until there was nothing left but a patch of charred ground, not even a white feather. The smaller children wept and there was a hush in the house all day.

Someone remarked that wasn't it strange that the white canary had died on the anniversary of poor Beatrix's strange disappearance?

THE EIGHTH TALE

KOIMÃO

KOIMÃO

A sunny, windy cemetery on an island off the West African coast. Everything is dusty, the air you breathe, the tall beaky bird of paradise flowers, the brown tunics of the monks, the straggling paths, the sparse shrubs. Far below, there is the sea. Up here on the mountain there are the graves. Koimão; they are all sleeping up here.

Although the month is January, the sun is hot. Its beams streak through the modern coloured glass windows of the chapel, sending blue, green, crimson, golden tongues of fire on to the plain brown coffin with its plainer lead cross lying in front of the altar. The chapel is tiny, Spanish-style, originally Spanish but now Spanish-for-foreigners. Everything is Spanish here, the language, the dust, the generally exhausted atmosphere. There are few mourners, some who cluster at the back and do not either sit or kneel down for they really don't know what is expected of them, others close to the coffin with its pathetic bunch of wilting red roses over the cross. The Requiem Mass is said hastily by a Spanish priest who waits for the responses and, when he does not get them, supplies them for himself. A little homily in English had been prepared but, due to some misunderstanding, is not read. All is over very quickly. The coffin is hoisted, after being sprinkled with holy water, into the waiting hearse by panting men from the undertakers - there is some discussion over tips, for no one knows quite what they expect - and then the hearse starts to crawl down the unweeded path as far as the little garden, once enclosed but now surrounded by crumbling walls, where so-called foreigners such as former Korean, Chinese and British residents are buried. They all stand in silence as the coffin is carried from the hearse to the burial niche, high up on one wall, pushed into it and sealed with a temporary asbestos cover, on to which a name is roughly painted. The surname doesn't fit, but it doesn't matter, they are assured. The wind blows their hair, the dust into their eyes, while a small priest called José Ramòn reads a brief burial service in halting English. Then they begin to walk away in a desultory fashion, some crying openly, some dabbing at their noses with their handkerchiefs, some chatting. But they all cast glances, as they pass through the one-time entrance to the walled garden, over the little enclosure with its quaint, beautiful Korean and Chinese gravestone inscriptions.

Now they stand outside the cemetery and look at one another. Most of them are somewhat dazed, for it had all taken so little time. They had expected something more. The cab-drivers, knowing better, had waited for them. "My God" says someone, "You must feel in need of a drink!" No one answers, for they are all rolling crazily one against the other as the taxi whirls drunkenly around the hairpin bends that lead down to the city, home, small comforts, life.

Within themselves, they all feel something like relief. They do all feel in need of a drink, and, if the truth is to be told, they all got rather drunk before lunch.

*

The whole island had been stark staring mad for the past twenty-four hours. The islanders, a mixture of Indians, Africans, Goans Portuguese and Spaniards with an admixture of English colonial blood and a large new colony of Indians, Pakistanis and Chinese, had begun to drink champagne and exchange Happy New Year and Happy New Love wishes several days before. Now she, the temporary foreigner, realised that New Year was to them the celebration of birth, the birth of another life, another chance, a chance to start again, and they were all gamblers. Fierce and fearless gamblers. Bingo had been imported and all the halls and hotel lounges were full, over-crowded, day and night; people sitting at tables gravely and in silence following the numbers illuminated on the gigantic wall boards. And how they drank! The evening before had been an African fertility rite, she thought (without ever having witnessed any such rite), for the whole night through people had danced in the streets, plunged into the tepid sea (sharks rarely crossed the coral barrier), had celebrated in the dirty streets. Everyone had at least one bottle. Old women, down at the port, had waved their bottles shouting "Buen Ano... Happy New Year"... and she had wondered, saddened as she was, what possible happiness could await them.

But now, at last, on the morning of New Year's Day, all was quiet. Not a soul was to be seen in town at ten o'clock in the morning. Most bars were closed except those whose proprietors were still too drunk to close them. The island slept profoundly, and the church bells called the faithful to Mass in vain. She walked along the deserted street, feeling happy in spite of everything, enjoying the sun, marvelling at the total silence. She thought of the raucous excitement of the day before. Today nothing moved, not even the wind.

A brilliant day of sunshine and promises. High up above the city, with at one end the ancient Spanish quarter dominated by the grim grey stone cathedral - the first building of the ancient Spanish city - now surrounded by clusters of houses become slums, and at the other end the recently built multistoried blocks of flats overlooking the harbour with its yachts, fishing boats, tankers, cruising ships, speedboats and flashing hydrofoils - high up above the city was the British hospital, and out of one of the front windows stared the woman. An hour before she had been walking along the deserted streets, enjoying the silence. Now she had entered into another universe, one of suffering, and often of death. To the right and left of her, greyish, flat-topped mountains curved into the sea-sky haze. As she stared down into the sparkling sea she counted the fishing boats, the tankers, watched those on the move and tried to reckon their speed. She tried to imagine the islands out there, unseen but there, tried to picture the African coast, not so far away. She also tried to place herself in a precise moment of time, and found it difficult.

Years before, she had stood in another hospital room, at another window, in another country. It had been another winter day of astounding brilliance. Another figure had been lying in the hospital bed. The bedcover had been bright yellow, like the sunlight. The sea beneath, a shimmering bay, had sparkled just as this other sea was sparkling now. And the figure in the bed had been lying still, couldn't sit up, couldn't see the beauty that lay beneath.

She had turned to the bed often, sat holding the woman's hand for long hours, poured out glasses of water which she had held to her lips. The sick woman asked repeatedly for tea, which was brought in often, but neither of them touched it. Then, at one point of that endless afternoon long ago, a knock had come to the door. A youngish doctor had come in with a suitcase which, when open, had proved to be packed with phials, needles and other apparatus. He had set about fixing up the drip while she had stood at the other side of the bed holding down the sick woman's night-dress in a perhaps foolish attempt to preserve some dignity for her. The sparse, grey pubic hair must not be exposed. Perhaps the youngish and, by his way of moving, effeminate doctor, sensed her anxiety, her insensate outrage.

"Your dear Maman" he had said, "Is very sick."

"I know" she had answered, "I know."

But she had never thought of death.

Now she turned back to the bed, to the sleeping figure, to the table cluttered with medicines, plastic drinking straws and an untouched glass of milk, to the chair in which she sat at the foot of the bed with her spectacles and the silly book she was reading lying on the sliding bed-table. She looked at the man sleeping in the bed, propped up by the pillows, his mighty head. the silky well brushed hair, the painfully thin body. She wondered, not for the first time, how he had ever come to end up here, in this semitropical island, the refuge of tourists and the retired, an exile from Africa where he had lived all his life as an expatriate, an exile from his roots, which he had no doubt refused. She thought of the brilliant youth and the parties, the safaris, the private nursing-home, the nannies and the native servants, the nurses who had adored him, the women in his life. It had all been a spectacular show, none of it true, none of it real. It had all been marvellous, but it had all been artificial. No really meaningful relationships had been formed. It had all meant nothing if now he was lying here alone dying, worried about money and pretending not to know what was wrong with him. Because of course he was pretending, pretending for everyone's sake. And they were all pretending, too, for his sake.

What a total lack of comprehension! Why couldn't people be more simple? She began to wonder if life ever had any sense.

He stirred, opened his eyes, saw her. She took his hand, his "good" hand, for the other one was paralysed.

"You had a nice sleep. Do you feel better? Do you feel like sitting up and looking down at the harbour? A lovely big cruising ship has come in."

"Eight o'clock" he managed to mouth with difficulty through dry lips, "It will leave at eight o'clock this evening."

"Smile" she said, once she had lowered him back on to his pillows. "Try. Just a little smile for your little sister. Go on, try".

He tried. She kissed his forehead, looked into his eyes. They were asking her for something. She knew what it was, and she didn't know what to do. But it was New Year's Day. She had only three more days on the island and then she had to leave. His eyes followed her as she moved to the little table, fixed on the bottles of medicine. She knew very well what he wanted. An old doctor, he wanted to cut loose before it became too bad. Before the dreadful thing that was killing him became intolerable.

She sat down, picked up the book. Wherever did you get this? I never read anything so depressing.

He made a gesture with his hand as if to say, I only pretend to read anyway. Then the door opened with a bang. The ward maid had brought in tea.

She poured out two cups and held one to his lips, but he shook his head. He couldn't swallow and was too tired to try. As she drank hers slowly she thought all the time, desperately, what am I to do?

Dusk was falling when the nurse came in. "Doctor Brown, a happy New Year! You're looking fine, in great form! I'm sorry I couldn't get in before to see you, but there's an emergency on. All the cirrhosis patients got drunk last night and we've got two or three heart cases and an attempted suicide. So we are a little busy. Why do people go on so at New Year? If they had a little consideration for doctors and nurses... eh, doctor? So will you give the doctor his medicine, Mrs Smith? You're an expert anyway. You know, the usual ten drops - he likes to count them - in two cc of mineral water. Thank-kkk --- you... and a happy New Year again to both of you!"

And in a moment she had disappeared, leaving her brightest Irish smile with them and they could hear the sound of her footsteps tapping softly down the rubber-paved floor.

For a moment, silence fell in the dusky room. But even in the half-dark, she knew that he was still looking at her, fixing her steadily with those great brown eyes of his. He was telling her to do it. She knew, she knew. And he knew that she knew. There had always been that silent conveyance of thought between them. She got up.

"Medicine then, all right. Doctor's orders. Let's count the drops together" she said, pouring some water into a glass and unscrewing the top of the medicine bottle. She moved over to the bedside. "One - two - three" she counted, and when she got to ten she raised her eyes and looked at him. He nodded his head. "Eleven - twelve - thirteen" and she got up to twenty. He nodded his head again. He wanted, she could see, to be sure. It didn't really take all that much, in his condition. She looked at him almost pleadingly. He shook his head, then nodded again. Tears came to her eyes. "Twenty-one - twenty-two twenty-three"... When she had got to thirty, he raised a finger. She went to the table and picked up a straw. She held the glass to his dry lips and slowly, slowly, he began, coughing at times, to suck.

When he had finished, she took the glass, threw away his straw, went into the bathroom and washed the glass thoroughly. She dried it carefully and placed it beside the medicine bottle, to which she added a little water. Then she sat down beside the bed, cradled his head and his poor swollen neck in her arms and, with her cheek on his forehead, fell asleep.

So did he. When they came in with supper, that was how they found them.

Down in the harbour the cruising ship, on the dot of eight o'clock, festooned with coloured lights, slowly moved out towards the open sea, disco music blaring. The town was similarly awake, and celebrating. Everyone was happy. Everyone had to be happy. After all, it was New Year's Day.

THE NINTH TALE

THE WAITING GAME

THE WAITING GAME

It was difficult to know where to begin - thought Kleist standing shivering in the cold January sunshine outside the plain square hospital edifice which strangely enough housed a "chapel"; it was difficult to know where to begin, at which precise point in human destiny the evil thing had taken over, had begun its inexorable march towards the extinction of the being which housed it. Two years ago? After the journey to Africa? Or had it been lying in wait, for years, until the right combination of biological factors occurred, to make itself manifest?

The wind was very cold, and the scattering of colleagues of the dead man, standing in isolated groups which in no way belied in-Service alliances, was evidently discomfited. To begin the year like this! most were thinking bitterly. To choose to die on the twenty-ninth of December! So that, on New Year's Day, when every normal person stays at home, surrounded by his loved ones if he has got any, eating and drinking to excess and warming himself by his fireside, they, just they of the Service, out of decency, had to turn out in the cold wind at three o'clock in the afternoon to attend Messmner's funeral service. What a beginning to the year!

Kleist was thinking much the same thing, but his thoughts wandered a little further than the self-protectionary limit, the self, the family, the inconvenience. Kleist had a certain predilection for thinking in the abstract: Man, Destiny, the Human Condition were concepts which appalled but at the same time fascinated him. Moreover, he was waiting for his wife to join him - she had known Messmner too and Messmner had made a lot of her - and he was hoping urgently that she would get there in time. The Chief of Service was already there, standing with his wife a little apart from the others as befitted his rank. Kleist, as new second-in-command since the untimely death of Messmner, would not have liked his wife to let him down. The Chief's wife, impassive, perfectly turned out, a black Persian lamb coat over black trousers, only a slight line of white showing at the neck, showed neither grief nor indeed any other emotion, except perhaps a faint but controlled annoyance. Her husband on the other hand, well wrapped in a dark tweed coat with a fur collar, was less unmoved. He seemed distressed, but then he was a very superstitious man, as Kleist knew. Kleist could guess at his feelings - exasperation and some fear. What a way to spend the afternoon of New Year's Day!

The widow, in the meantime, was nowhere to be seen. She must be already inside the chapel, supposed Kleist. And the children with her. Strange how little widows count, he thought, in a way, on their greatest occasion. A widower - well, that is another story, surmises as to possible remarriage - at fifty-odd a man is good for at least another twenty years, how well he is bearing up - poor woman, she always did her best! But a widow is quite another thing. To start with, the very sight of her reminds all males present of the unpleasant possibility of their wives being in her position. And then as a rule she is plain, bedraggled, unkempt - too many tears have undone years of beauty treatments, and at least for the moment, she doesn't care any more. Then, if, as in the case of Messmner's widow, she has been reasonably well provided for, the general public sees no real reason for her grief, which is taken to be in good measure hysterical, or else a desperate appeal for commiseration which no one feels actually to be her due.

In the midst of these considerations, Kleist saw his wife's small car appear and he waved to her with a feeling of relief which was, perhaps, in the circumstances, excessive. He disguised this at once under a show of elaborate signs as to where and how to park, and hastened, trying to walk slowly, to greet her.

She too, descending from the car, seemed distressed. Although she was neatly, even smartly dressed, her make-up was badly applied, as Kleist noticed at once, and as he pointed out to her. "I haven't got a handkerchief" she whispered, "give me one." Kleist pulled a paper tissue out of his pocket - not that he normally used the things but he had had a bad cold recently - and waited silently while she removed the smudges around her lips. "I was in such a hurry" she explained in apology, "I didn't want to be late." Kleist suppressed an exclamation of annoyance. He didn't want his wife to apologise to him. He only wanted her to be perfect. She didn't seem to realise that men don't want to know everything about women. It brings them too close to them.

As they rounded the corner a small group of mourners began to move into the chapel. "They are going in" said Kleist, suddenly agitated, "let's follow them."

A long dark corridor faced them on entry. This was the hospital morgue, and nothing about it resembled a chapel or church of any kind. Kleist pushed his wife ahead of him and followed her unsteadily down the corridor. Suddenly she stopped. "Do you think this is him?" she said urgently, absurdly, standing outside the open door of a darkened room in which could be distinguished only a white bier with the body of a man laid out on it, shrunken, arms crossed, face blackening. "No no" said Kleist, trying to get her away, "He is already in his coffin."

Indeed the coffin was there, to the right of the room which acted as a chapel, a huge bunch of white flowers on top of it. The funeral service began. Surrounded by the dead waiting to be buried, surrounding Messmner's coffin, the small congregation seemed in some ghostly manner to be celebrating its own survival. "Requiem in pace" intoned the priest. but is there peace there? wondered Kleist. Standing behind his wife, he thought of the years he had spent in an office beside that of Messmner, thought of the times they had had lunch together, thought of his life-long resentment of the man, his conviction that Messmner was deliberately obscuring his, Kleist's, merits, of his contempt for what he had years before defined to himself as Messmner's womanish ways. He thought of Messmner's mane of white hair, his mania for hygiene, his collection of stamps and his diets, his childish capacity for enjoyment. Kleist had never been able to enjoy life, he was of too pessimistic a turn of mind, but he had always envied those who did.

And then the rot - the evil thing had taken over and Messmner, now become "poor" Messmner, had gone into hospital, and people spoke in hushed voices of leukaemia, and they all knew that there was nothing more to be done for Messmner. He had come out of hospital, however, and everyone had congratulated him without being really convinced, he had gone back to his office, but he hadn't been able to keep it up, at four in the afternoon he was already tired out, even driving his car had become too much for him. Then the decayed tooth, the antibiotics, the relapses, the return to hospitals, the talk of a "stabilised crisis", then the last news - the Last Rites, coma, agony, death. And that, thought Kleist in something like amazement, could happen to me! It could happen to any of us here, only the others don't believe it. A slight swelling of the glands, nothing at all, a certain unaccountable exhaustion, tests, tests, more tests, spells in hospitals, recovery, convalescence, hope, illusion, suddenly ill again, back to hospital... and you end up in a coffin with your dear colleagues around you, all of them wishing they were somewhere else.

Now the priest was speaking of Messmner, removed from the toil and stress of life, safe in the bosom of the Father. He circled the coffin with the sprinkler from which the holy water dropped. Messmner had never been religious, thought Kleist, I don't believe he had ever been in a church since the day of his first communion, except, of course, to get married. I wonder what he is making of all this now? Admitted that Messmner could still make something of anything.

The priest withdrew and the widow was helped out of the first pew, supported on either side by her children, who seemed undecided as to the part they were supposed to play. They were deeply embarrassed of course and perhaps that was their main emotion. As Kleist had supposed, the widow was by now quite unrecognisable. Hair streamed untidily from under a black veil which sat askew, black stockings made her legs look old and wizened, her face was swollen, deformed by tears. She bent to kiss the coffin and almost fell on it. Then, with what was a stifled scream, she was almost dragged away and out of the chapel, past the dead awaiting their turn, out into the cold bright sunshine. "Rather excessive" murmured someone behind Kleist, "After all, everyone was expecting it." Kleist turned round angrily. As he had expected, the speaker was Bloom, a relative newcomer to the Service. "Grief is never excessive" Kleist said through his teeth, "Remember that, Bloom, it is never excessive enough."

Bloom's astonished face swam in front of him, disappeared. Kleist's wife took him gently by the arm. "I was close to him for so many years" he whispered to her hoarsely, "Even hating a person is a link" he added, surprised by his own perspicacity. His wife, seeming not to hear, drew him towards the coffin from which the attendant had already removed the flowers, and looking at him steadily for a moment, she turned and laid her hand upon it. "A last good-bye" she said. "A last good-bye" thought Kleist, and then an atrocious doubt almost deprived him of breath, had there been anything, anything real between them? But it was too horrible a thought to harbour, another reason for hating Messmner, and now he didn't want to hate for, at least in that brief space of time, he realised the futility of hatred. Exhausted, he fell on his knees and prayed for a fair deal, if such a thing exists in eternity, for Messmner.

Outside, there was a long empty pause. Everyone was doing their best to return to normal. The groups had little to say to each other. People stared into the bright, terse January sky. Kleist at one point shook hands with the widow His wife was embraced by her although she did not seem to remember who she was. "What are we waiting for?" said someone finally. "For the hearse" answered Kleist. "The hearse is late. We can't let the coffin leave alone. I mean, we can't. And then the widow won't leave before her... husband."

Time passed. The sky, at first tinged with pink, grew grey and the wind became colder. The groups formed and re-formed. Old ladies, unperturbed by the event, shook their heads and spoke of journeys in foreign lands, where certain diseases were rife. The widow wept on other shoulders. Friends of Messmner spoke of the past and the future. Kleist and his wife approached the unmoving couple, the Chief of Service and his wife, and there was a brief, cold exchange.

After an hour or so the Chief of Service, grey in the face, said that unfortunately he had to be getting home, urgent work was waiting for him. Certainly the undertakers had blundered. Had someone telephoned? However, eventually - but someone would wait, Kleist must delegate someone to wait. The coffin could not leave alone. Kleist no, he could not spare Kleist in the circumstances, Kleist must come home with him, they would have a stiff brandy together, they certainly needed one after all this, and then they could get down to discussing the new situation.

Kleist brushed his wife's cheek. She looked at him compassionately and turned to where her car was parked. The chauffeur opened the door of the Chief of Service's limousine for Kleist and, he, under a fur rug, with the Chief of Service's wife laughing beside him in her low throaty laugh, could almost forget. Almost.

THE TENTH TALE

LIKE GOING BACK

LIKE GOING BACK

She had been alone all afternoon, typing letters. She had smoked an incredible quantity of cigarettes, filling the blue and white chipped ashtray with butts, one of which fumed and smoked angrily as, emptying the lot into a crumpled sheet of carbon paper, she tidied sketchily before going to change her skirt and put some make-up on.

To post her letters she would have to go into town. A nuisance. She really ought to have a bath and change, but it seemed too much trouble. Who would see her, notice, pay her a compliment? She would take the dog for company. Already he had sensed an outing, and was looking at her expectantly.

The new car took some minutes to warm up, but it moved smoothly enough into gear. She had everything, she had checked before closing the front door - her purse (on occasion she had gone out without money) her keys, her letters. It was that time of day she liked best, when daylight was fading into dusk. The trees of the villa had turned a deeper green, the poppies were dark smudges of scarlet in the long grass. Over the Janiculum, past the fountain she never stopped at and the breath-taking view she could never more than glance at briefly. One day she must stop, look, saunter, breathe deeply. Surely, over the years there would be time? Down into Trastevere, the cobbled streets; careful at this blind corner where children are always playing. Past the bar and the butcher's shop, the church of Santa Dorotea where she had heard mass on her mother's first anniversary, sad, huddled, baroque. Now on the upsweep, on to Lungotevere, the long wide carriageway that skirts the river, into the flow of traffic, undisciplined but skilful, cars gliding smoothly, weaving between the lanes; a fast-moving school of piranhas. Stop at the traffic lights, turn left on to the bridge. The river muddily gleamed, the cupolas clustered on the skyline softly shone. Rome was a beautiful city, she so seldom noticed it. Put the sidelights on, most cars have got then on already. The first approach of night, a pity. If one could say stop! fix the moment, live no more... time must have a stop, but it never does. How banal. How many people have said that in how many different ways? Impossible to be an original thinker. Still, it was something one felt, therefore valid, no? More traffic lights, only two cigarettes left, can't bear the thought of another she thought as she took one out of the packet and groped for her lighter, but she lit it all the same. Now cars coming from all directions, mingling in a seething mass, miraculously extricating themselves and heading off in all directions once more. How clever Italian drivers were, graceful, yes they drove gracefully. Out of the corner of her eye she saw her husband's car parked at the usual place. Should she go to see him in his office? For a moment she slowed, undecided, then put her foot down on the accelerator once more. He might not be there, he might not be pleased, anyway she had no time. These sentimental impulses she still had... did he ever experience them, these days?

They had been married for a long time, nearly twenty years. They had both changed, but he much more so than she. That was normal, she supposed. Other women put up with it better, though. Or found other interests. Or had lovers. She had never had a lover; it would have been more sensible. She had never been sensible, just... faithful... to what? To an image formed twenty years before, of which nothing remained? To an institution? To a habit? Was it so important? She found herself questioning everything these days, even her own identity.

How changed her views were from what they had once been, she thought as she steered carefully up a narrow street lined with closely parked cars on both sides. At the top of the street, when she was about to turn right, a tiny Fiat started to move out without showing a signal. Angrily, she blew the klaxon. The fair girl driving the Fiat started, looked at her and smiled apologetically. At once she felt her anger recede, and she smiled back guiltily. Must she be everyone's governess?

At last she saw a car moving out and swiftly slid into the empty space. Just room, thank goodness. She locked the doors carefully and, with the letters in her hand, began to walk along the narrow, crowded pavement towards the post office.

There was a queue at the counter. She joined it. Ahead of her was a bronzed woman wearing dark glasses, holding a letter addressed to Tripoli. Ex-fascist, she thought, anyone who has anything to do with Tripoli must have been a fascist! The Mussolini epoch. He hadn't done so much harm, only one big mistake, the war. It wasn't really fair to bracket him, as her countrymen always did, with Hitler.

There was a great difference between the Latin and the Teutonic temperaments. The Latins could also be bestially cruel, but passionately so. They were more humane. More humanely cruel? Is it better to be humanely cruel than... But surely there is no such thing as humane cruelty?

A man to her left was holding a letter for Bucharest. She took a swift glance at his face. Deeply bronzed, dark bushy eyebrows turning white, probably a Rumanian. Not a difficult language to read. Once she had managed to read nearly a page of it in the civic library. A Latin language, after all. A common heritage. Whose common heritage? The role apportioned to her at birth had been that of an outsider. Since the age of ten, when they sent her to boarding school, she had watched other people living. Now her own life seemed to her that of someone else. She had always been an out person.

A small thin old man with a pointed beard and a beret and a tattered briefcase was now handing over a letter addressed in beautiful, flowing script. She could not read the address, not even the country. Russia, perhaps? He must be a Russian émigré, perhaps a painter, though that was too obvious a guess. He took a used little purse out of his briefcase to look for change. Worn, the purse, like its owner. A poor old man. Did he skimp, and save, and walk back to his lodgings rather than take the bus?

When she came out into the warm square, the street lamps were on. It was ten to eight, the shops were about to close. She hesitated. She ought to go straight back home, the children had gone out and perhaps had not taken their keys - but she was so seldom in town; it would be nice to walk through the crowded streets. Ten minutes would not make much difference. She started off, paused at the church door, decided not to go in. The flower-seller at the corner was still there, but the blowsy woman who used to produce packets of contraband cigarettes from somewhere under her skirt had gone. No more contraband cigarettes; now everyone has enough money to buy their cigarettes legally, over the counter. A pity. It was more fun in the old days.

She went into the big brightly lit café, walked past the counters where under glass were all sorts of tempting delicacies. They look better than they taste. All these solemn people, eating sandwiches on drug-store high stools, where were they on their way to? This place was better in the old days too. In the old days there were small, round marble-topped tables, and dark corners, and old silent-footed waiters who knew you and didn't try to hurry you up over your coffee. She drank her cool drink quickly. It was very cold, in a tall glass with a clean white napkin under it. Some grace was left, although now that tips were forbidden the waiters treated you with indifference. She moved so as to get a glimpse of herself in the mirror behind the counter. What sort of image did she project? As she did so she noticed a man who was looking at her fixedly, and, suddenly flustered, she paid and walked quickly out of the glass door.

She made her way into the square, and was about to start up the narrow street where she had parked the car when she saw the book shop. Everywhere else was closed. She might find something interesting. It was a discount book shop which advertised a 50% reduction on every book it sold. She walked along peering at rows of remainders, successful and unsuccessful, novels, art books, nothing that took her fancy. The Karma Sutra, of course; she had flipped through it once in a book shop in Paris. Asked for a great deal of effort - and Fanny Hill; a pity her favourite remark was mostly unquotable: "If I had read it twenty years ago my life would have been very different. I would have known what to look for."

Poetry: Eliott, Pavese. Was it true that Pavese killed himself in despair over his sexual inadequacy? Vercelli, Poems 1945 - 1965. Vercelli! She reached out, good, one of the copies was free of its cellophane wrapping. The title page bore his name, Michele Vercelli. She turned the book over, read the critical notices, the biographical introduction. Paris in the post-war years on the wave of the new realism, the people's realism: politically committed, three novels, plays, poems. Now held a chair at the University of... , sponsored an experimental theatre... on the jury of several literary prizes.

Obviously Vercelli has gone bourgeois, she thought, going in for all that he used to condemn. Amusing, almost. She began to read the poems. They really aren't all that good, she thought, just the occasional lyric mood, the occasional bright image. They were mostly addressed to women. Perhaps she would find one addressed to herself. No, one to a black goddess. Well, coloured women as well! Thank God she hadn't slept with him. Frowsty hotel rooms, doubtful sheets, the smell of smoke and sweat and semen... "Why won't you/ Take what I offer/ Pylon, tree-trunk, obelisk/My sweet and violent love." It might well have been.

She finished the poems, confirmed in her opinion of years before. He wasn't a great poet. A small talent like her own. Should she buy the book? No, pointless. Suddenly, remembering the time, she moved away, she must get home. It was half-past eight. Those eternal discussions at café tables, over meals, in the Luxembourg Gardens, had always ended with her going home alone. For a few weeks she had troubled him with her refusal. Stale old arguments he had used insistently. "Have the courage to live, free yourself. Come with me, I promise you joy. I can give you joy." She had always laughed, never taking him seriously, never believing that what he was saying applied to her. For to her it was such a big thing, she couldn't believe that he was serious. That must have been it. She was a real innocent, let loose in a far from innocent world.

It would be fun to meet him again, now that she was a different person. Perhaps in a publisher's office. Michele? *Ciaò!* You don't remember me?

An English girl in Paris, studying. You said you were in love with me. We used to talk. You wanted me to translate your first play. The first time we met as in that little restaurant, Rue des Canelles. Ah, now you remember! I see you've turned bourgeois. No? Hungary put you off in 1956, did it? And you left the Party. Is that why you've changed your publisher? We might meet sometime, you say, if I'm free. I'm never free, don't you remember? I've changed, have I? Well, so have you. You were thinner then, and you had a hungrier look about you. And now you're almost bald. But still attractive. Yes, I'd like to see you again.

She was back at the car, opening the door, turning the ignition key. Put out your signal, they never do here, I don't believe they ever use their driving mirrors, they teach far too much theory in their driving schools, why don't they teach them how to drive. Anyone who has learned to drive in England can really say they can drive. Smoothly, out into the street, don't push anyone out of his place but take your opportunity. It all boils down to a question of good manners. Let other people know what you are about to do. Like a game of bridge. Signals.

Passing a hotel on the Corso, she thought, and if he asked me to sleep with him now? Would my refusal be so steady, so amused? I think, she told herself, I think I would say yes. He would be surprised. He would say, what's become of your principles then? I would answer very smoothly, nothing has happened to them, I still have them, I am just going to betray them for once, that's all. And for the first time too, only of course you won't believe me. I am going to let you make love to me; I mean it - but coldly, out of curiosity, like a man. No emotion involved. You couldn't, he would mock, you can't do anything without emotion. I'm learning, she would answer, truthfully, I'm doing my best to learn. Men can sleep around and still come back to their wives. Why shouldn't women? It's like going back to work when the children are grown up and you feel you have a little time left before retiring. I want to make love to you out of curiosity. I want to know what I missed, or didn't miss, years ago. I want to know if my life, lived my way, has been worth while. I want to know if I was right or wrong, don't you understand? God, you still don't know yourself, he would say. You are a sensual woman, but you were always afraid of men, afraid of life. You were too well brought up, that was it, you didn't know that life existed. You never slept in the same bed with your parents and heard them coupling, you never saw the alley-cats at it. You were brainwashed by religion, by the respectability of a small town. You had enough discernment to know that the way of life you were born into wasn't for you, but you never had the courage to go the whole way, to take a lover, find out, discover yourself. It's too late now, you know, if you have found the courage it is too late.

Not courage, she would correct him, just curiosity, and you always attracted me you know. Or perhaps you are right, perhaps I didn't have the courage then, and now it doesn't matter.

You can 'phone me, she would tell him, when you're in town. You must be careful, though, very careful... my husband, the children. I'm theirs, you see, they own me in a way, or think they do... Well, you think you own your husband, don't you? he would say and she would have to answer, yes I do.

You have had women ten times more beautiful than me, she would tell him at one of their meetings. I'm not at all beautiful, although I can make myself seem so. It's all due to excitement, and make-up. Was I beautiful then? You had the head of a Greek boy, he would say, as he used to, and the figure of a boy too. But you don't make love like a boy.

And they would start loving again. She hoped he wouldn't smell. He had been scruffy in the old days, but in a romantic, wild-cat way.

Once he had besieged her, literally, for about a week, coming to her hotel every day, twice a day, to leave notes, flowers. She had enjoyed being in her ivory tower. When she had seen him, finally, it had been to tell him that she was going away, back to England to visit her family. He had been so downcast that she had allowed him to come to her room, but only to watch her packing. He had been very tender, very reverent. *"Ma petite vierge"* he had said when they said good-bye and he had kissed her. What a nauseous part she had played! Had she had a Virgin Mary complex or something? Had she always been such a nauseous person?

But in her own justification, she reminded herself, she had not loved him and her senses had not yet been awakened. Yet she had felt a bit of a heroine.

The car had brought her home without her noticing it. She saw her husband's car parked in the drive. God, was it so late then? She was flooded with a sudden feeling of guilt. For a moment she almost believed that she was coming home from an assignment in some dusty hotel room.

She couldn't resist it. While they were having a quick drink before dinner, guess what I saw in town! She said. A book of poems by Michele Vercelli. Do you remember the name, she risked. She remembered the copy of Vercelli's first novel with its dedication to her which had disappeared from their bookshelves. So he's still going strong. The poems are pretty feeble, though. He's gone all bourgeois, on the jury of this and that, left the Party...

"Your old boyfriend!" said her husband without taking his eyes from the television. He didn't seem particularly interested. She got up slowly, rather sadly. So it didn't matter, really.

THE ELEVENTH TALE

UNCLE POPPY'S PICNIC

OR

THE RUNAWAY WIFE

UNCLE POPPY'S PICNIC
OR
THE RUNAWAY WIFE

Looking back cn the day, I could fairly describe it as one of the most fantastic I have ever spent. When we arrived this morning at Uncle Poppy's villa we found three other cars already there, and Uncle Poppy himself, in white ducks and a Panama hat, holding court in the garden. This 'garden is in reality a little plantation of orange and lemon trees. I was solemnly taken for a tour of it by Uncle Poppy himself, who wanted to show the *'straniera'* his exotic cedar-lemon tree. From this sacred tree an enormous cedar-lemon was plucked, I thought at first for me, but no, it had to be divided into three parts by Uncle Poppy, using his huge pocket knife: one part went to the gardener who had cared for the tree, one part to Uncle Poppy, the proprietor, and the third part was presented to me, the guest. After this ceremony we were taken into the house where we found another guest hiding behind an armchair. A little bald-headed man, he was dragged into the open and introduced to us by Uncle Poppy as his 'American cousin'. He seemed very withdrawing, doing his best all the time to hide the lower part of his body behind something, and certainly his little white old man's legs did not show to advantage in bright blue Bermuda shorts. Don, G's wittiest cousin, told us afterwards that the Bermudas had been forced upon him by Uncle Poppy. "Whatever Uncle Poppy says he must do, he does" said Don. "Uncle Poppy tries to go too far to see if just once he refuses, but he never does." The little old man's name was Alfredo, and he was not, it turned out, a cousin at all; however, Uncle Poppy was conferring an honour on him by calling him one.

A bedraggled woman with children clinging to her skirts was also introduced by Uncle Poppy; I shook her damp hand, to her obvious surprise. Not until afterwards did I realise that she was the 'parasite maid' as the cousins called her. Apparently she, with her children, husband and in-laws, lived with Uncle Poppy to 'look after' him, and lived 'on' him very satisfactorily.

When the procession of cars set off we had no idea where we were going, but were simply told to follow. The journey seemed long, and beach after beach was passed with groans from cousins, wives and guests. At last we reached what is probably the only really bare and uninviting stretch of beach in Sicily; here the first car turned off the road and bumped down a sandy track for several hundred metres, to stop beside a kind of shack where some felt-hatted peasants were eating bread and grapes. This was the picnic site, we were told; Uncle Poppy parleyed with the peasants, who disappeared, leaving the shack at our disposal for the operation of changing into bathing costumes. Rather bad-temperedly we did so. Uncle Poppy was really going too far. I observed a large fish in a vine-leaf covered basket being taken out of the first car by the 'parasite' and her daughter; I wondered idly what the fish was doing here, but it never struck me that it was to form the substance of our picnic.

The sea, however, was blue and sparkling and warm as always in Sicily; when we emerged from it to sit and smoke on the beach we found Uncle Poppy, in ancient swimming trunks, stretched out full length on the sand with a nylon stocking on his head, being covered in warm sand by the adolescent daughter of the parasite maid. This, he informed us, was the reason for which once a year he came to the sea. Warm sand baths were good for his rheumatism. There was nothing like warm sand. He urged Cousin Alfredo to borrow a nylon stocking for his head and follow suit. This time, however, Cousin Alfredo put up some resistance, but he would certainly have weakened and in the end given in had not the signal for lunch been given.

Lunch, it seemed, was to be eaten in the shack among the long grass where we had changed. We found enormous circular dishes of *'timballo'* waiting to be divided among us; this is a kind of huge 'cake' the basis of which is pasta layered with minced meat, cheese and tomato sauce. It was certainly very good. I had two portions of it, hoping to avoid the fish which was roasting on the ashes of a small wood fire, tended by the parasite and her daughter. Flasks of Uncle Poppy's own wine were circulated. Conversation was varied, and always seemed to be more interesting where one was not; I found myself beside Cousin Alfredo who talked to me non-stop in execrable Italo-American about the Bronx, where it appeared he lived when not in Sicily. Since he praised without reserve everything that was American I soon got bored and signalled to G. to come and rescue me. G. came over, sat down, and did no rescuing at all. He was fascinated by Cousin Alfredo, and drew him out even more.

After lunch the picnic was considered over, and we were told to get back into our cars. This time, however, a halt was conceded, at a fountain which might have been Uncle Poppy's own, so emphatically did he promise us the best water we had ever drunk.

Everything with Uncle Poppy is shrouded in mystery; he loves to promise surprises, each one of which will be, he is sure, better than the one that went before it. The fountain turned out to be a roadside one where several lorry drivers had already pulled up. G. was engaged, at one end of the long trough through which the water flowed from the rock into another at a lower level, in washing the sand from his feet when a lorry driver came up to him and asked him in a very reasonable tone if he thought it hygienic to wash his feet in the water which other people, below, were innocently drinking. G., who had not realised that the water in the upper trough flowed down into the lower, agreed that the lorry driver had a point and hastily withdrew his feet to the accompaniment of much laughter.

Once back at Uncle Poppy's villa the cousins dispersed, but we were bidden to stay there for the siesta. We were taken upstairs to a room with painted walls, an arched, painted ceiling and Louis XIII white-painted furniture; this was to be our place of rest. We spent the afternoon on the lumpy bed talking about Uncle Poppy, who was sitting downstairs under the pergola with Cousin Alfredo and a bottle of brandy which was rapidly diminishing between them.

Uncle Poppy had never worked, said G. His life had been spent more or less as we had seen today, surrounded by relations, dependants, servants, always bent on making an impression. This had been his bedroom when he was married. Was he a widower then? I wanted to know. No. said G., his wife ran away with a bank clerk and since then he has never set foot in this room. The bank clerk was the greatest offence his wife could have committed. Was she still alive? I asked. As far as was known said G., yes, in some other town in Sicily. And were they divorced or separated? Of course not, said G. Uncle Poppy disapproved of both separation and divorce. If one were to be left, betrayed, as he had been - well, that was another thing. He had behaved as an honourable man, *'un uomo d'onore'* He had ignored the whole episode, and had done exactly nothing.

G, then fell asleep and I spent the afternoon restlessly staring at the painted ceiling and speculating as to the runaway wife. Had Uncle Poppy just bored her? Had he, in his honourable way, been unfaithful to her? Had the stagnation overcome her and so she had made a bid for escape?

She too must have lain sleepless on this bed staring at the ceiling, a sleeping husband beside her.

Anyway, she had got away.

THE TWELFTH TALE

IL MAFIOSO

IL MAFIOSO

It had been a cloudy, overhung day, with some rare drops of hot, sandy rain. The beach had been deserted in the morning. Only English and German au pair girls, who called to their charges in shrill voices and between themselves lapsed into the accents of New Cross and the home counties, Hamburg and Bavaria, shared the tepid, and not very inviting sea with us.

The evening was no better. We were exhausted with travel, and the weather; but it was Saturday night, and something had to be done. Besides, our stay was to be a short one.

The dinner party was arranged about eight forty-five, by telephone. No one could make up their mind about the restaurant. It had been that sort of a day. However, a choice would eventually be made. That is the way things happen in southern countries.

We met our dinner companions at the Rotonda. When our car drew up there, a quarter of an hour late, a tall, heavy figure detached itself from the shadows. A mane of white hair topped a sardonic face, out of which two coal-black eyes gleamed, now with amusement, now with rage. This was Doctor L., once, we had been told, one of the best surgeons in the country but who had long since retired from the medical profession in a fit of spleen. He didn't like the way things were run, and since his wife was wealthy, and he was wealthy, it was really all the same to him as far as money went: and he had the satisfaction of telling the medical profession to go to hell.

Doctor L. was not at all put out by our lack of punctuality. His wife was sitting in their car at some little distance, surrounded by passing friends who had stopped for a chat. We were introduced to her, a fine-looking woman of about forty, stiff and regal in a plaster cast which swathed her from bosom to thigh. We were introduced to the friends: hands were kissed, hands were shaken, polite words were exchanged. At last we drove away.

"We have decided on 'The Pirate'" said our cousin. "It's a new place, We've been there twice, and eaten well; the L's have been there once and eaten badly. The chances are on us eating well."

"The Pirate", although well-lit, was completely empty. Perched on a rocky plateau overlooking the sea, the edifice bore some external resemblance to a ship and inside gleamed with polished brass, upturned barrels, little bars and low beams. A maître d'hôtel in a spotless white jacket stood chatting with two young waiters as we entered somewhat diffidently. Rows of light oak tables shone, small coloured lights twinkled, the sea stealthily lapped the pebbly beach below. No one paid any attention to us.

"I said we would have been better to try the 'Sirenetta' said our female cousin. "This place is too empty. Why don't we go away?"

But no, we had arrived, and the effort necessary to climb back into the cars and drive somewhere else seemed too much to all of us. We waited by the copper-topped bar.

Eventually one of the young waiters became aware of our presence. He led us to a table, which he then proceeded to set with knives and forks, glasses, napkins, everything but a tablecloth.

"What about the tablecloth?" asked Doctor L., who had been observing the table-setting operation ironically, in a dangerously pleasant tone of voice.

The young waiter pretended not to hear.

"What about the tablecloth?" suddenly thundered Doctor L., in such tones that the maître d'hôtel came scurrying.

"Are there no tablecloths?" demanded Doctor L. of this individual. The maître d'hôtel said that yes, there was one tablecloth but that with polished tables they did not use....

"Put it on the table!" roared Doctor L.

The knives and forks, the glasses and napkins, all were whipped off with extraordinary speed and a white tablecloth was laid. The maître d'hôtel extracted a pencil and notebook, snapped his fingers at one of the young waiters to bring up the fish trolley, cocked his head and waited.

"We'll have two bottles of Corvo 1967," said Doctor L.

One of the young waiters sidled up behind the maître and whispered something.

"I regret, sir, there in no Corvol" said the maître. "We have an excellent white Chianti 1971."

Doctor L. shrugged his massive shoulders, made an expressive gesture with both mouth and hands, and in a tired voice requested a cigarette.

I must say that the mussel soup - when it arrived - was really excellent. The mussels were fat, juicy, enormous. My only problem was how to use fingers and fork while keeping my scarf decently arranged over a décolleté which, I realised now, was attracting Doctor L's smouldering attention.

Doctor L., between mouthfuls, declared that the land was rotten, and the peasants likewise. He assured me, as a foreigner, that a people accustomed to the whip needed the whip and that without it we had the results I was unfortunately observing that evening. .

The real trouble began with the fish. Our cousin A. and Doctor L. had chosen, as experts, two shining silvery *orata* to be grilled for them slowly over hot coals and brought to table with salt, pepper and browned butter as their only garnish. When, after another half-hour, the fish arrived and the two plates were placed in front of the gentlemen, there ensued a brief period of silence. Doctor L. raised his bushy eyebrows and interrogated our cousin A.

"If this is *orata,* A., you are either going blind or you can't tell one fish from another."

A., in his turn, glared over his spectacles at the maître d'hôtel. Then, with some difficulty, since he really prefers silence to speech, he finally said:

"This is not *orata*. I chose two *orata* from the trolley. This is *saracò*. Where have our *orata* gone?"

The maître, seeing himself in difficulties, summoned the two young waiters. Had there been any *orata* on the trolley? The young waiters assured him that there had not.

"And yet I chose *orata*" said our cousin A. "A deep-sea fisherman can't mistake *saracò* for *orata*."

The fact was undeniable, and the maître sent for the cook. The cook declared that not only had he not had any *orata* in his kitchen that day, but that no order for *orata* had reached him.

At this point Doctor L., who had been looking at the fish on his plate and the maître, the cook and the waiters with unparalleled disgust, roared:

"Take it away!"

No amends could be made. The maître, now close to tears, proposed all the other dishes he could think of: Doctor L. was not to be moved. The maître then broke down and told us that it was his first evening as maître, his first evening at 'The Pirate', and that if we did not condescend to overlook the débâcle it would be probably his last.

Doctor L. told him to give him some slices of cheese.

At that moment the padrone entered, a short man whose belly stretched his tight white shirt and overhung his tight belt. He had a parcel of tablecloths under his arm. He chose that unfortunate moment to enquire how our dinner was proceeding.

Doctor L. refused to answer but went on munching his cheese stoically. Our cousin A. explained that there had been some occult substitution of fish. The padrone frowned and summoned the maître, the young waiters, the cook. Explanations were many, but no one ever mentioned the true one: that the *orata* had gone to another table. The restaurant had filled up a little since our arrival.

The padrone seized the notebook and pencil from the maître, and announced that he, personally, would take our next order. What should it be? Fresh fruit salad with ice cream: they had all flavours.

Orders were varied and varied flavours of ice cream were requested. When the padrone left us he handed over his bundle of tablecloths to the young waiters who proceeded to put them on all the tables. We looked at our watches: it was close on midnight. Could he be expecting a big party at that time? Or was he merely demonstrating that he had tablecloths, after all?

The delay this time was very long indeed. We wondered if they had gone into town to fetch the ice cream, and if they were cutting up the fruit for the fruit salad. Doctor L. said that again that the whip was the only thing and that he intended buying a mare and retiring to the country. Mrs L. said that that was all very well, but that she had no intention of retiring to the country with him. She also reminded him that although he talked of the whip, when it came to defending his wife when she was insulted by an insolent shopkeeper, he seemed to have nothing to say. Doctor L. said that in the first place he had not been present at the moment of the insult, and that in the second the insolent shopkeeper had been one of his dearest school friends, more, a blood brother, and that no woman would ever come between them. Mrs L. said that was just what she meant. At this moment the ice cream appeared.

It could not be seen, buried under mounds of little brown biscuits. Although various flavours had been ordered, each little dish was half-filled with the same white, milky liquid. Doctor L. stirred his spoon among the biscuits, eyed the padrone who was hovering nearby, looked round at all of us, took out his wallet, yelled for the bill, slammed two or three large notes on the table, and delivered himself of the following:

"Don Amerigo! If ever you should see me setting foot in your restaurant again, kindly ignore me or turn me out, for once bitten, twice shy, and the third time means that one can't take enough punishment."

The padrone protested: Doctor L. was giving him great pain. The maître hovered with a bottle of whisky and green glasses in his hands: all to no avail. Like the hippopotamus rising from the mud, Doctor L. rose from the table. We all rose, and followed him.

"And yet" I ventured once we were outside, for after all I remembered that we were guests, "The mussel soup was very good." No one paid any attention to me. Words were insufficient.

We reached the villa before the L's who came later. "More trouble!" said Mrs L. triumphantly. Doctor L. heaved his great length and bulk into a seat, stretched out his legs in front of him and requested a cigarette.

"In the nervous condition in which I found myself" he said at last, "I would have smashed his car to bits for him. Driving with my lights on, of course he saw me coming! Drove right up to me, and waited for me to back! A whippersnapper of a young chap, with a little Fiat 500. 'Didn't you see my lights?' I asked him. 'No' he said, 'I saw no lights.' 'Then you've no business to be driving' I told him. 'And if you don't back out of this lane pretty smartly, I'll tell you another thing: I'll ram your car, and smash it into scrap-iron. My nerves had reached that point, you see, Smash it into scrap-iron! He could see by my face that I would have done just that, so he nipped back into his car and backed out like lightening. That's the power of money for you!"

"But, excuse me" I said, somewhat confused, "If you had rammed his car, wouldn't he have called the police? And then... wouldn't you have had damages to pay? Or even perhaps prison?"

He laughed heartily, his long sardonic mouth twisting with amusement at the idea of prison.

"That's what I have been trying to explain to you, dear lady" he said, bowing. "There's a great deal of talk about the power of the intelligence, the power of the working classes, the power of this and of that, but there's only one power that counts, and that's the power of money! It might have cost me a million, that's true, but what's a million to the satisfaction of showing an insolent jackass just what real power is? The power of money! That's power for you. The power of money!"

He said no more that evening, but seemed to be ruminating, his eyes slits in the clouds of his cigarette smoke. The L's left quite early.

Next morning, when we arrived at the L's private beach for a swim, Dr. L., majestic and impressive in a striped bath-robe, asked us, guffawing, if we had had indigestion from our dinner of the night before. He was concerned, he protested, in case we had over-eaten.

THE THIRTEENTH TALE

MOTHERS

MOTHERS

The cat woman sat there in her hairdresser's chair staring at herself moodily in the mirror, blue eyes glittering with heavy shadow with little sparkles in it, her high round cheeks puckered, her dark hair screwed up in tufts of cotton wool, her skin the colour of pale mud. Several heavy gold, diamond-studded rings lay on the glass shelf in front of her beside her cigarettes and gold lighter. The girl in the short yellow shift putting lotion on her highlights admired them. Were they real? she wondered. The cat woman laughed. Of course they were real. Her voice was deep and hoarse and her accent broad. "Souvenirs" she said. "Presents... although some of them I bought myself. I like the feel of them on my fingers. And I like gold. Men admire a woman with a lot of rings. Classy, you know. What's that? Another time dearie, I'm going to be stuck here all day it looks like. What time is it? When will you let me out?" She turned in appeal to Gianni who was dealing deftly with about twelve heads. "I have to 'phone, Gianni. I have to give a time for an appointment this evening." Gianni shook his head. "As soon as possible. Today I'm alone. See all these people? Are you in a hurry?" he asked without irony, ignoring the obvious.

"And then there's my son I have to find out if he's home from school. I have to find out if he's all right, doing his homework. You know how it is, Gianni. Children. Sons and daughters." Gianni shook his head again. "You mothers" he said with a tiny moue. The cat woman shrugged as if he couldn't possibly understand. "What else have we got?" she asked, half-closing her slits of eyes. "Tell me, Gianni."

On the other side of the salon, staring gloomily at the cat woman in the big mirror sat the jump-suit lady, consulting her watch every two minutes.

"Really Gianni" in a tone of reproachful, restrained annoyance, "You are neglecting me today. I was here before your other client. I have been here since... " She began to collect her things. "Four-fifteen exactly, right after my aerobic class, Really, Gianni..."

Exasperated, Gianni bawled "shampoo!"

The jump-suit lady went to the wash-basins, still pouting.

Concetta and Maria were cousins. They had grown up together in a town in the south of Italy, and gone to school together, had been in the same class. They were daughters of two sisters and even the houses they lived in were in the same street, as were those of their mothers, their uncles and aunts and their grand-parents.

They were already engaged when they left school and they got married at a distance of some months, to two boys who had gone to their school. Augusto and Mario were the sons of two brothers. There was a discreet rivalry over the weddings for, since one followed the other closely, comparisons were unavoidable. Maria had a romantic dress, all lace and flounces and a long veil, Concetta a short white silk suit and hat. The cost of the wedding breakfasts was more or less the same, although the menus varied. Concetta's father had provided a flat for his daughter, Maria's likewise although in both cases it meant running into debt.

The husbands were 'good' boys, provincial and swaggering, really too young for marriage, despotic in public towards their wives, aping the behaviour of older married cousins and friends. Concetta and Maria were acquired objects, not expected to pronounce themselves in the presence of others, to stay at home as much as possible and to see to it that their husbands lacked for nothing. Both girls accepted their men's attitude, considering it to be 'normal'. They had expected this type of treatment once they had become engaged, let alone married. They had seen it meted out to their mothers, their aunts, their grandmothers. Why, should they be different?

Concetta, who had married first, was the first to expect a baby. Ever since the day she had got married people had been asking her with a certain under-current of malice if she had any 'news' and, after three months, she could at last answer "yes". There was some commotion in the two families directly involved. The first grand-child! The two mothers-in-law made arrangements to take some of the housework off her shoulders, to go to cook for poor Augusto if poor Concetta did not feel up to it. Concetta allowed things to take their course.

Maria watched all the fuss with some jealousy, for she too had a right to her moment of glory. However, after a month or two she also was able to make her triumphant announcement. And so both young women grew big, shopped for maternity clothes and confided their trials and troubles to one another. Their mothers and husbands looked on, basking in the general approval.

Two and a half months after one another two baby girls were born. In the families there was great rejoicing, although the respective fathers were silently commiserated with since the newly born children were not boys. But later on, this deficiency was made good by the birth of other children to both couples, and life went on at a jog-trot rhythm made up of births, christenings, First Communions, marriages and funerals.

Augusto, Concetta's husband, was a well-to-do *'piazzista'* or commercial traveller, so he was away from home from two to four days every week. He had his adventures, more or less as everyone expected him to, but there was one type of adventure of which he was ashamed. The temptation was too strong for him, the desire too great to be resisted. It was only in his cousin Mario that he felt he could confide. He was drawn irresistibly to little girls just on the threshold of puberty. It was like being very thirsty and wanting to drink fresh water. You couldn't stop yourself. Mario, listening to his confession, was not so surprised as he might have been. There was nothing unusual in liking little girls. Some men liked other men. Some liked sheep or goats. Men were allowed, socially, practically any type of sexual mores, as long as they were prudent. Men were men, givers of life; they could, in theory, give life to anything. There was no written law that said they could give life only to their own species.

Mario, in consequence advised Augusto to walk carefully. "Keep well away from home" he said. "Don't touch any of the town girls. Anyway, you travel a lot don't you? Not that anyone would believe the kids if they did talk, you being a respectable married man and all. But you know how it is. When mud is thrown, some of it sticks."

One hot summer day the two little cousins Angela and Stella were playing in the garden at the back of the house that had replaced Concetta's original flat. They were both ten years old by this time, pretty and precocious. They had not begun to menstruate yet, but they would very soon. They knew all about it, of course - no avoidable surprises were in store for them. Angela was taller and thinner, with straight hair and a less timid air than Stella whose black curly hair and liquid eyes reminded one of a little black furry animal always ready to jump up and run away. Angela was better at school,

Stella was too frightened to stand up well to oral interrogation. They were playing at one of their favourite games, making up, each dressing the other's hair in turns, applying rouge, lipstick, mascara and above all eye-shadow. Augusto, watching them from the porch, thought how pretty they were and what a pity it was that some other man would enjoy them before long. The thought passed through his mind almost unconsciously, shocking himself as it did. But it was a thought that was not to leave him either that day or those that followed. Gradually he became obsessed with his daughter and his niece and took to buying them little presents, asking them about their boyfriends, warning them to be careful when they were with boys. Neither Concetta nor Maria noticed anything. Concetta thought that at last Augusto was beginning to take some real interest in his family. Anyway, both she and Maria were taking driving lessons, and she was pleased not to have to leave the children quite alone while she was away.

In the course of the summer, Augusto's obsession grew. He wove a kind of complicity between his daughter and himself that was unaware and innocent on her side, wily on his. He would take her out to the shops and buy her clothes and shoes. He bought her a bikini which Concetta thought was just this side of decent. Then he would talk to her for hours, asking her if she knew what went on between girls and boys, doing everything to win her confidence, bring her out, to make her talk about herself.

In this way from high summer the months passed until September came around.

Stella had come to stay with Angela because Concetta was away -- she had had to go into hospital for a day or two for a small gynaecological operation. Once Concetta had gone, Augusto began to lay his plans. The time had come. He was like a man crazed, with no real knowledge of what he was doing. First he took the two girls to the cinema, to a film which made them blush and titter. Then they went to a restaurant and he poured them each a glass of wine. When they got home, it was not too difficult to get them into the big bed with him, where the two children left their virginity and Augusto behaved like a pig.

Next morning, the two children woke up to find themselves alone. Augusto had vanished, while in the rest of the house could be heard the noise of the other children's departures for school. The cleaning woman, who came in three times a week, was, they supposed, in the kitchen. Once the reality of the experience of the night had dawned on them they began to cry, Stella sobbing hysterically. They held on to each other tightly. When they recovered enough to move in the bed, it was to find the sheet blood-stained in several places. They were aghast. Finally Angela gained the courage to slip out of bed. She found, pinned to the door, a crudely executed drawing, in elementary-school style, of a little girl with pig-tails, her mouth open as if she were about to scream, but in the mouth there was a round stone. "What's that?" whispered Stella. "It's a warning" replied Angela, tearing the drawing from the door. "It means we are not to open our mouths. Remember, Stella - something awful will happen if we do."

They got dressed, went through to the kitchen and got through two bowls of white coffee and bread. The cleaning woman asked why they had missed school. "We overslept" answered Angela, quite truthfully. "Stella was sleeping with us to keep me company because Mama is not here and we talked until it was late and this morning we didn't hear the alarm."

When Concetta came home she was a little surprised to find that Augusto had disappeared, but she took it that he had been summoned unexpectedly by his firm for some reason. After a week he did turn up; drunk, unshaven, unlike himself. Concetta helped him to bed and called up Maria to tell her the news. "He's very odd" she said. "I can't think what he's been up to. If he's been having an adventure, it hasn't turned out well."

Maria said let him get over it, what do you care anyway, you know what men are like, as long as the money comes in --- and, by the way, when are we going to take the driving test? She and Concetta went to the school that afternoon, fixed the date for the test, went to the hairdressers, had an ice cream at the new café in the town square and then left for their respective homes. Augusto was still in bed when Concetta got in, around seven-thirty. He didn't want to see her. He wanted nothing to eat. Concetta was disconcerted. For at least a week her husband lay in bed in the darkened room, his mind in a state of complete confusion. He had raped his daughter and his niece, had taken off before sunrise for Messina, had spent a week in various brothels, most of the time more drunk than sober. Now what was he to do? There was only one way out. Try to act normally and above all keep everything quiet.

It wasn't so easy, though. Concetta would get - if she hadn't already - suspicious if he kept sleeping in the spare room. She was worried, he could see that. She kept urging him to see a doctor, and there was no illness he could think of to explain his odd behaviour. In the end he decided that he needed a long break. He would persuade his employers to send him on a market research survey to the north of Italy, calling at the retailers of the products he sold, to hear how they were selling and how sales could be improved. It would take him away for at least a month.

Concetta let him go, not without some anxiety, for although their relationship was a very loose one indeed by this time he was still the father of her children, still the head of the house. However, he left her plenty of money to be going on with, and said he would phone her from time to time. The oddest thing about him though was that he would hardly look at his daughter Angela. This was such a change in his behaviour that Concetta was dumbfounded. The climax came when he was leaving the house for his trip. Angela happened to come into the hall on her way to school and Augusto turned his face away in order not to see her. He seemed to be suffocating.

Concetta asked him if he was feeling all right, if it might not be better to put off his departure for an hour or two but he said no, he would miss the morning ferry from Messina, he was all right, it was just the emotion and he had had a nasty turn, that was all.

To go back. The greatest problem had been getting rid of the sheet. Angela had had several problems to face on that particular morning she and her cousin had woken up in her parents' bed - one, for instance, was trying to calm down the hysterical Stella - but the blood-sticky sheet presented the most immediate and alarming of all. Angela had thought a lot about it. She could put it in the washing machine - but the cleaning woman would have seen it; she would also have wondered why she was interfering with the household duties which normally were none of her business. She could have tried to wash it herself by hand but she could never have got it clean. The only thing that remained to do was to destroy it - by burning? Someone would see the smoke and wonder what was going on. To bury it? This seemed the best of all solutions to Angela, who hid the sheet in a drawer, put another on her mother's bed and, in the late afternoon, when the cleaning woman had gone, took the sheet out and ran with it quickly into the garden.

It was that part of the garden which had been turned into a small vineyard. She dug a hole, deep enough she thought, under a very old plant that had been there when they bought the house and never gave any fruit, She imagined that the worms, attracted by the smell of blood, would come soon and eat the sheet - no doubt the taste and smell of blood was a pleasant one to the worms. So she finished digging her hole and stuffed the sheet into it, covered it up with earth that she padded down and ran quickly into the house.

When Concetta came home, nothing serious had happened, nothing had been done to her really but the removal of a couple of small benign growths, but since she still felt something of an invalid, she lay down in a deck-chair on the back porch after lunch. Friski, her little terrier dog, was with her. He soon scampered down beneath the porch into the vineyard and proceeded to dig something up. Concetta, from her deck-chair, took it to be a bone. But the dog started pulling and dragging - something once white, covered with earth and dark with blood - something very long and white which, in the end, proved to be a sheet. A sheet with several bloodstains on it. Concetta got up quickly from her deck-chair and went down to look more closely. It was indeed a sheet, and the bloodstains were really there.

She thought deeply, if frantically. It was a sheet for a double bed, therefore, even if Angela had begun to menstruate it would never have been on her single bed. It was one of Concetta's own sheets, modern, flowered and with elasticated corners. She had bought it when out shopping with Maria. Who had been in her bed in her absence was the question that throbbed in Concetta's head? She began to think of Angela. Angela was not a stupid child - far from it - and if anything had been going on in her mother's absence she would have noticed. So just what had been going on? Stella had come to stay. Now the two children, the sheet, Augusto's oddness and his prolonged absence began to form in Concetta's brain into a hard coagulated mass of certainty.

Augusto had been up to something - but what?

She suddenly remembered the day before, when at the sight of Angela he had turned away and hidden his face. Oh God! Not that! Concetta's blood seemed to freeze in her veins. Not that, oh God, not that!

She began to remember the protracted chats, the buying of new clothes, the bikini, the big change, in fact, from the bored and uncaring father of before to the over-caring father of recent months. Oh God, it had to be that!

She went inside to the telephone calmly and called Maria. "Maria" she said with her usual authority. "Take Stella to your gynaecologist. Or else take her to the old midwife, my mother's friend. She won't talk." Maria at the other end of the line was at a loss for words. "What?" she said. "What have you found out? What has she been up to?" "She hasn't been up to anything" said Concetta coldly. "She has been interfered with, I swear to God. Both of them have. Stella and Angela. I haven't seen Angela yet. She hasn't come home from school. But I know.

"But who?" asked Maria, in anguish. "Who?"

"I think I know that too" said Concetta simply. "Ciao" and she put down the receiver.

Angela, cross-examined and confronted with the sheet, broke down. Yes, it had been Daddy. Yes, Daddy had been acting in a funny way during the past months. He had been - how to say it - almost courting her. She had been pleased, at first - how many girls' fathers took them out to buy clothes? - but when Mama went into hospital she had begun to get worried, that was why she wanted Stella to sleep with her and then - when Daddy took them into the big bed and started undressing she hadn't known what to do or whom to turn to. And Mama wasn't there...

Once Stella had heard from her mother that Angela had told everything, she too told her story. At the midwife's she had refused to talk. She had sworn never to breathe a word to a living soul. But then Angela released her from her promise. They hadn't meant to go to bed with Uncle. He had put them there. And he had looked so strange as if he were mad or something. She had been afraid he was going to kill them. Boys of their own age never did things like that, although there were some girls at school, older girls.... And then Aunt Concetta hadn't been there.

Come October, Augusto had still not reappeared. He phoned now and again - from Milan, Turin, Vercelli, Verona. It was already getting cold in the north, he said. He would be home soon. After this telephone call Concetta rang Maria up. "Maria" she said "Do you know where Mario keeps his pistol?" For most men in the town kept a firearm of some sort in the house. "Of course" said Maria. "In the drawer of his bedside table. Thieves, you know. Prowlers". "Ask him if it is loaded" said Concetta. "Tell him to show you how to use it. Tell him there are rumours circulating of daylight burglaries. Tell him you are scared. All right? Once you have talked to him let me know." Concetta put down the receiver. She already knew how to use Augusto's pistol - he had shown her himself, since he was away so often. It wasn't difficult to shoot somebody especially at close range. The main thing was not to lose your nerve. Concetta thought that perhaps she ought to have been a man. But then, if all the women like her had been men, what would the other women be?

Maria called her a day or two later to say that Mario had loaded his gun and given her a rudimentary lesson in using it. Concetta approved. "Practise a bit" she advised. "If no one's about. Practise shooting into a pillow. Try and hit the same spot over and over again."

At the end of October Augusto came home. He was in poor shape, had lost weight and even his hair had got thinner. He blamed it on the cooking he had had to put up with, far away from home. You couldn't get a decent plate of pasta in Milan, he said. It was rice, rice all the time. Perhaps there was something wrong with his liver. Now and again he got sharp abdominal pains. Perhaps he would go to a specialist and have a check-up. Concetta agreed that this was a good idea and added "Before you go to the doctor, Augusto, do let's go out for a day. We, haven' t been out for years. Let's go to the country and eat in a trattoria and have a walk in the woods. Perhaps there are still some mushrooms left, late ones. Maria and I can do the driving, if you don't feel up to it. I hope you trust us. Anyway you can see how we drive and give us some hints. You know we both took our driving test, months ago. The examiner said we were both very good drivers for women." Augusto, with a faint smile, agreed. The outing was fixed for the coming Sunday. Mario would not be there since he was going to visit his father in hospital.

Concetta insisted on the front seat. While Augusto drove, she sat beside him. Then she took over and drove until they reached a trattoria near some woods where they stopped and had a good meal well washed down with wine. Augusto seemed to feel relieved to find himself alone with his wife and her cousin. They were comforting women, he thought, not like the others who always wanted something, love or money or flattery or all three. Concetta and Maria, he thought complacently, if a little foggily, were the best women in the world, apart from his mother of course. A man likes to be comfortable with women, to be able to confide in them - well almost if not completely - to feel friendly towards them, as if they were men. In this pleasantly euphoric state of mind he climbed into the car, asking Maria to drive since he was sleepy. They would drive closer to the woods and then go looking for mushrooms.

On the edge of the wood Maria stopped the car where the track ended. Augusto aroused himself from a doze to ask "Is it here? We get out here?" He said no more, for the cold nozzle of a gun was sticking into the base of his skull. In the split second before it went off Augusto knew why. He knew why and he forgave, he was grateful to, he admired Concetta. It was right. It had had to happen. Then he slumped into the bucket seat with a dark trickle of blood staining his white shirt collar. Now Maria in the driving seat turned to him. She fired straight into his heart. Augusto's body leapt in the air and subsided. The two women got out of the car, pushing past the body, walked round and opened Augusto's door. Almost simultaneously they fired at the corpse's genitals.

By now he was pretty well cut up.

Concetta said briefly "I'll drive." They were both breathing deeply. Maria got into the back seat, covered the body with a rug and they drove fast into town, straight to the police station. Here they got out and went inside. "Take the body that's in the car outside" Concetta said with authority. "He was my husband. He wasn't a bad man really, but... he was a man. Like yourselves. We are not sorry for what we have done. It was right. It had to be done. It could not be avoided."

They are still awaiting trial. They are respected in their block of the women's prison. They are serene, hardworking and unworried about anything except their children.

*

"Mothers!" said Gianni, shaking his head.   "Thank God I have only one."

"You see," purred the cat woman, "Some people have two. Like balls, Gianni, like balls."